EATING ASHES

EATING ASHES

A NOVEL

BRENDA NAVARRO

TRANSLATED BY Megan McDowell

Liveright Publishing Corporation

A Division of W. W. Norton & Company
Independent Publishers Since 1923

For Norma and Angélica, my two moms

First published in Mexico in 2021 by Editorial
Sexto Piso, S.A. DE C.V as *Ceniza en la boca*

For information about permission to reproduce selections from this book,
write to Permissions, Liveright Publishing Corporation, a division of
W. W. Norton & Company, Inc., 500 Fifth Avenue, New York, NY 10110

For information about special discounts for bulk purchases, please contact
W. W. Norton Special Sales at specialsales@wwnorton.com
or 800-233-4830

Manufacturing by Lakeside Book Company
Book design by Brooke Koven
Production manager: Louise Mattarelliano

ISBN 978-1-324-09608-5

Liveright Publishing Corporation, 500 Fifth Avenue, New York, NY 10110
www.wwnorton.com

W. W. Norton & Company Ltd., 15 Carlisle Street, London W1D 3BS

Authorized EU representative: EAS, Mustamäe tee 50, 10621 Tallinn, Estonia

10 9 8 7 6 5 4 3 2 1

PART ONE

I think I take myself too serious
It's not that serious
—"SYMPATHY," VAMPIRE WEEKEND

I DIDN'T SEE IT MYSELF, but it's as if I had, because I feel it drilling into my head and I can't sleep at night. Always the same image: Diego falls and his body hits the ground. Then I wake up and think, this didn't happen to me, it didn't happen to Jimena, or to Marina or Eleonora. It happened to Diego. And over and over, the sound in my head, a smashing, like a window shattering or driving into a sandbag, thud, no warning. Dry, definitive, a violent collision of ribs, lungs, and concrete. Like this: boom. No, like this: boooom. No, like this: crack. No, like this: drack, drackut. No, like this: baaam, clap, crash, broooom, bruuuum, gruuum, grr, groo . . . and an echo. No, there is no word to convey the sound that it made. A body smashing against the ground. Diego wanting to be thunder, wanting to interrupt the music of his body. Diego leaving us just like that, but still hovering above us. Diego, starstuck, a smash hit.

I didn't see it. My mom didn't see it. We were both far away. Mom farther than me, because she had left us long before Diego killed himself. My mother, nine years away.

When Diego was five years old, he thought of our mother as being up in the sky, and whenever a plane passed overhead he would say: Look, it's Mom up there. That's not Mom, dummy, I'd tell him, but Diego insisted that it was and he'd wave to her and then when she called he'd say: Mom, did you see me waving at you yesterday? And Mom: Yes, I saw you. And what were

5

you doing? he'd ask. Oh, well, I was looking at you, whenever I'm about to fly over the house, I go to the window and wave at you. Did you see me waving back at you? And Diego, grinning his gap-toothed grin, would say: Yeah, I saw you.

So you want to be a pilot so you can work up in the sky with Mom? No, I want to fly alone, without a plane: just me in the air, no cape. Well, you can't do that. Yes, I can. No, you can't. Yes, I can. No Diego, you can't fly. Yes, I can. And Diego could, for a few moments: six seconds. At least, that was the estimate of the neighbor across the way who'd watched the fall before turning to tell his wife to call the police. Six seconds. You *could* fly, Diego, for six seconds. From the fifth floor to the sidewalk. Six seconds, little brother. You can do it all.

Are you thinking of me? Are you thinking? No, Diego, you can't be thinking of me, because you're dead.

ALRIGHT, LET'S HAVE A CHAT. Sit. You have to be strong, because you're all grown up now, right? Yes, yes you are. I'm going to leave and you two are going to stay, but it won't be forever. Nothing is forever, I've told you that before: it's just for a little while, then you'll come live with me and everything will be better. No, don't make that face, that's exactly the face I don't want to see you make. Do you have to cry over everything? I need to leave because, well, what am I doing here in Mexico? Yes, I know I said that the last time, but last time was different. It was different because it was different. You were different, I was different. But you know what doesn't change? Exactly, you keep eating more every day. Get it? Sure, you get it, you understand perfectly. Have you thought about Diego? So little, so helpless, so good. Just look at him. When you were his age you were already playing on your own, but this one's so dependent, he's like his father, just like him, except not *just* like him, because we're going to raise this one to be different, right? And that's where you come in. It has to be you, who else can I trust? My mother? Your granddad? I need to trust you and you need to trust me. Enough with the *oh woe is me, I don't know what I want*. Maybe you don't know, but no one does, and that's just how it is. You're going to help me because it's only by helping each other that we can help ourselves. What you do today, what you decide today, is going to help you tomorrow. Right? And that's why you're not going to make a scene and that's why you're going to be very good and every day you're going to wake up and say, Yes, this is what we need. Or do you want to go on like this forever, in this room, in this house, this city? You don't want that. Even if you think you do, you don't.

And I didn't say a thing, didn't cry, didn't say yes, didn't say no. My mom and her soliloquies, Mom being Mom. And then she left. One Monday morning, while Diego was still asleep. Shhh, she said, keep quiet, or you'll wake him. And I scowled at her, scowled hard, as if my eyes could communicate everything she wouldn't let me say. I hate you and you hate me, and we hate each other, and you hate my brother and how he keeps you awake all night, and you hate everything: you hate yourself and my grandparents and your dead husband and me. You hate me and that's why you're leaving me with your son, and that's why you act like butter wouldn't melt in your mouth, but really, you're already picturing yourself on the plane, you're already on the plane, you selfish jerk, you're already there. You're already picturing yourself all European, all sophisticated, strutting right onto that plane. And I said all of that with my eyes, but my lips were pressed together and my stomach was clenched up, like it wanted to fuse with my intestines and join in their endless goddam gurgle gurgle.

Give me a kiss, she said, bringing her cheek close to mine, and it felt cold but soft. Because my mom was always cold. She was so thin and so hypoglycemic that she always had a cold body, and, I imagined, a cold heart. Come on, she urged, and she brought her cheek to mine again and I made a kissing sound: *mwah*! Then I sighed. She patted my shoulder and stared straight into my eyes: We're going to see each other again, you and Diego are going to come to Madrid to be with me and everything will be different. Better and different. Everything always gets better and different.

Right? And she left . . . And I saw that she had forgotten her earrings, the ones she always wore, and I picked them up and went outside to see if the taxi was still there so I could give them to her, but it wasn't, it was already gone. I was about to start crying, but Diego cried first and I ran to his bed to pick him up and I thanked him for being a little kid who didn't yet know how to ask questions.

I T WASN'T A SHORT TIME, MOM. It was nine years. That's what I told my mother when she tried to convince herself that life had played a dirty trick on her. Yes, it *was* a short time, it was the time that it took. Or you think you just arrive here and the king of Spain is waiting to greet you at the airport: Hi there, welcome, how are you today, please, come right in, we've been waiting for you? No. It was a short time compared to the people who have it harder; not everyone can do this, flights cost a lot of money. Or what, you think I can just say: Oh, I'm already starving, but now I'll eat even less, while they're over there gorging on the euros I send them? Or what, you think I don't know you two took advantage of me and extorted me and made me say yes to everything you asked for because I was far away?

You didn't say yes to everything, Mom. You always said no when we asked you to come see us at Christmas. You didn't come, but you did go on trips, you did travel through Spain while we were waiting for Diego to fall asleep on those nights when he was upset because you didn't call him. You didn't say yes to everything, Mom, because a lot of times I asked for your permission to go out with friends and you called and sent messages and wanted to know where I was all the time and I told you to leave me alone, that there were more than eleven thousand kilometers between us, and still I had you breathing down my neck. And you said no, that you weren't going to leave me alone, because women get killed, they get raped, they get kidnapped, and that's why you were going to bring us here. And now look at us.

And were you raped, were you kidnapped, was your body found in the Remedios River, is your face on a "missing" poster? No. You're still here. That's what she said, always the same sermon. And she flopped face-down on the bed to cry like Diego when he was five years old and I had to stand over him and tell him that's enough now, calm down, that he had to take a bath, and he would shove me away and tell me I wasn't his mom, and he'd keep crying until I got sick of it and offered him candy, and then he'd look at me differently and say ok, fine, but what was the point of taking a bath when in no time at all he was just going to get dirty again?

And that's what my mom got stuck on: How long, how long? How much time did I really have with him? And it was true that it hadn't been much: She didn't even get two thousand days with Diego. His first three years of life, plus the time he lived in Madrid. That's what my mother had: five years total with Diego. But still, I didn't believe that life had played any dirty tricks on her. Didn't matter how good a mother she was or wasn't, didn't matter how good and devoted a worker, life didn't cheat her, not when it came to Diego, or to Spain, or to me.

It was true, though, that she'd had a hard life. Not like Aunt Carmela, who had someone to support her and take care of her and shower her with luxuries. Not like my grandmother, who was all, I hate you, my husband, but then cooked him mole and purslane whenever he asked and told him that was love. No, my mom was the ugliest in her family, the awkward, dull one. Not like her sister Carmela, who my grandparents boasted about because she was blond, or like Aunt Margarita, my uncle's wife, who wore tight leggings so people could get a good look at that round ass of hers. No, people really called my mom ugly: big broad nose, dark skin, thick but shapeless lips. Skinny, squat. But also ugly in her voice, ugly in her sense of humor, everything ugly. And that's why when she got married to Diego's dad, everyone was happy and we all wanted a party and for her to wear white: because it was her moment. Her time to shine. That's why we danced and sang and put flowers in her hair and my grandfather took out a loan from the bank and we set up tables and chairs and a white tent in the yard and my grandmother ordered carnitas from Michoacán and hired a lady to make tortillas on a hotplate, and Abuela herself made salsa and charred the chiles and made sure that the music was loud and that everyone knew her daughter was getting married. And the groom, what a husband, they all said, so good, so hardworking, so stoic, so tame. Full salary, nine-to-five job, the perfect spermatozoid to make Diego.

And we went on like that for two years, two, until the man was diagnosed with cancer and wasted away in just a few months. Boom, out of nowhere, overnight: one day, everyone was happy; the next day, all sad. And my grandfather's house turned dark, or at least that's how it seemed to me: darker, dirtier, more normal. An average house with some average grandparents, with a mother who wasn't just ugly but also depressed, and I didn't have anyone to play with, except for Diego, who was tied to my apron strings.

I HARDLY REMEMBER anything about my mom's husband, just two or three scenes, and it's better that way. The last time I saw him, he was at his parents' house and my mom took us to visit him. I stayed in the yard and saw him come out of his room, and he wasn't my mom's husband, but the ghost of my mother's husband. Like that, the words in that order. A ghost. I didn't want to go upstairs and see him because it made me sad, and I didn't want Diego to go up either. I never saw him again. They didn't take us to the funeral, or even tell me when he died. I found out later, when my mom came back to my grandparents' house and went straight to bed. What about Diego? I asked her. Don't you want to see Diego? But my mom said no, she couldn't see Diego, because Diego was the spitting image of his father, which was true. And then my grandmother would watch Diego, and my grandfather would take me out to buy books or to the movies. And so on, almost every day, until one day we came back from the Wednesday market with our walnut and vanilla malts and our hundred grams of chocolate candies and the fruit for the week and we didn't find Mom in her room, and Abuela's suitcase was missing. She's gone! my grandmother said, with all the anger I would experience for myself years later when my mother left for Madrid. That bitch took off and left us her kids! And my grandfather told me to go watch TV and to take Diego too, and Diego and I sat down and watched the same movie three times in a row, and then we asked for a different one and they put on a different one, and we went on like that for about two months, watching movies all the time, until school started up and we got used to not seeing Mom. How much time passed before she came back, only to leave again? I don't remember, just like I don't remember her husband, or what I was like back then. And it doesn't matter, in any case, because I was already broken and I'd started not to hear.

FAIR—LIFE HAD NEVER BEEN *FAIR*. Not in our house, not with my mom as a single mom. Clearly someone had taken pity on her and then taken her virginity, and she'd gotten knocked right up. Or so my grandmother said—obviously my mom got pregnant her first time, right, because of course no sane person would want to get *her* pregnant. But what really happened, who is my dad? Your dad, well, your grandfather is your dad, because he's the one who takes care of you, because he feeds you, because he brings home the bacon, my grandmother told me. But not a word about my actual father. Who was he, what was he like, how did it happen? I don't know, Abuela said, and she mused aloud: I think she was raped. That's what I think happened, you see how your mom is, how she doesn't talk about it and keeps her lips sealed tight and gets mad if anyone asks her. I believe she was raped, and the poor thing thinks she has to carry that weight all on her own; I always want to tell her, just say it, there's nothing wrong with saying it out loud, and I'll listen. But if she did tell you, what would you say? I asked. Well, I don't know what I'd say, but I would say something, ok? You'd hug her, right? I asked. Well sure, of course I'd hug her, and of course I would tell her it's ok, don't worry, that I'm here for her, she doesn't have to suffer alone, and not to hate you, not to think that you're like the man who made you. Maybe that's what I'd say. And would you ask her if she knows who he is? And when I asked that question, my grandmother would get mad and start waving her arms. You dumb brat, I'm telling you your mother was raped and all you can do is keep asking who your father is? So what if you don't have a dad? Have you had to go without anything? Love, affection, toys, food? Why do you want to know who your father is, what difference would it make? And I lowered my head because I didn't know, but I wanted to know. I don't know what I want to know, but I want to know, I told her. And then she went back to the same thing: I think she was raped, I think that's what happened, but as you can see your mom doesn't say anything and keeps her mouth zipped. You know, when I was thirteen years old and my dad let the neighbors rape me, he told me better the neighbors than someone else we didn't even know, and I thought it *was* ok but it wasn't, because after that I was afraid of them all and never wanted a man by my side, but then your granddad came along and said he'd take me as I was, just like that, and my dad said ok, and your granddad told me it wasn't such a big deal, that nothing was ever a big deal, and that I should get it into my head that life wasn't fair, and he gave me two daughters and a son. Without asking permission, but with love. I love you, he told me, I touch you because I love you, and I cried and told him yes, it was ok. And that's why I think your mom was raped, but she doesn't say anything and you know she never will. She never opens up, and that's life: mothers want to hug their wounded daughters, and the wounded daughters won't let themselves be hugged.

And I thought my grandmother was right, that life *wasn't* fair, but it hadn't played any dirty tricks on anyone, at least not my mom, who never let herself be hugged and who never hugged anyone. Maybe Diego got played, Diego who left, who didn't say goodbye, who knew that life wasn't fair, but who didn't wait around for me to hug him. We weren't raped, little brother, no one inflicted horrible suffering on us like the kind you see on the news, our dinghy didn't capsize, we weren't beaten, we never had any videos of people yelling at us go viral, we had simply been hurt, and that was as close as we got to being like all those people we supposedly resembled.

WHEN THE POLICE come they're always too soon, but not this time. You can't trust time. Something like that was what I heard at first over the phone, but I wasn't understanding a word. What are you saying, who is this? It's about Diego, do you live on such and such street, at such and such address, floor, apartment number? Yes, yes, that's where I live. Who is this, what's happened to Diego? Silence. Dear, where is your mother? And I repeated: What's wrong?

And my whole body at that moment was a dry and almost gravelly whirlwind, the kind that blows dust into your eyes, that stings and blinds you and makes you cover your face with your hands and leaves your whole being exposed. And wham: the wind like a punch. And wham: disaster walloping your legs and torso and hair and me with my hands over my eyes because the dust cloud won't let up. Boom, bam, crash. Blow after blow, fast, like a boxer. The news of my brother's death by KO. Not two, not three falls. Just one. His. Dear, are you there? And the damned sand in my eyes, and my body going a thousand miles per hour, and the person on the other end of the phone line. Dear, are you there, and your mother, how can we reach your mom? Grrrrr, groooom, my stomach. Always my stomach: in the English test to prove I could understand just as much as Spanish people could (though they were surprised to find I knew more), there I was with my bad stomach, half an hour in the bathroom so I had less time to fill out the answer sheet and the woman from the Ministry thought I was being sketchy and even asked for my phone so I couldn't cheat. My bad stomach the first day Mom left for Spain: there I was, in the bathroom all day and then drinking chamomile tea that my grandfather made for me. Or the day Diego got sick and had a fever and I thought it was my fault because it was the first time my grandparents left me home alone with him. My stomach. Diego, you stay there and watch TV! shouting with the bathroom door open because my goddamn stomach. And so on, always, my stomach. Gurgle gurgle. Like a hollow sound trying to surface, clamoring for attention. Yes, I'm here, what happened? No, I don't know where my mom is.

DIEGO LIKED VAMPIRE WEEKEND. He listened to all their albums. Or at least I think he did. Or I imagine he did. Or that's what I want to believe he listened to before dying. Or that's what I figured when I saw his phone. Or that's what I dreamed those first days: Diego falling to the honeyed, catchy tunes of his favorite band. Diego singing and jumping in his mind, playful, playing us all: I'm outta here, assholes, you can't catch me. And the song in the background, like a music video. Let Diego have laughed, let Diego be music and let his flight have been a moment of mischief, trick or treat, the "If you don't gimme, I'll jump," or the "Come on, you're not my mom," and his impish little giggle to make me chase him. Diego: the chords, riffs, guitars, the drumrolls. Diego: the voice, the energy that moves Ezra Koenig's vocal cords, the sound that comes out while I watch the singer on the screen with the computer on mute. Diego, the definition of something, but not pain. I can't stand to stand his pain. Diego: music, not silence.

HOW PEOPLE USED TO call him Cule. Not Culé, like a Barcelona fan, but Cule, since Diego called everyone "culero" because he thought they were all assholes, but no one understood his South American slang, until they did understand and then they all thought it was an asshole move to call everyone an asshole. El Cule. That's apparently what they called him at school. El Cule killed himself. What's that about Cule? How, what? Was it because Bolivia bullied him, or because in music class the teacher told him not to lean against the wall because his hair left a greasy spot? Was it because sometimes he didn't have money and he was still hungry after his sandwich? What for, why? they asked, but no one knew and Diego became murmurs in the minute of silence they held in his classroom, a rueful rumor because, deep down, even if he was like that, the way he was, different, asshole-ish, silent, hot-tempered, he was still a good person. El Cule became good, a good person, ipso facto, to later become a meme . . . To later become a joke, to later become punchline and laughter: "Don't kill yourself like Cule," "This dumbass is crying like Cule," "Pinches Mexicanos culeros, güey, ¿a poco no?, ¡ándale, ándele, arriba arriba! Órale, güey." And laughter, Diego became asshole-ish laughter, and maybe that was exactly what Diego wanted.

Still, what can a teenager really want? How can we trust his word when he says one thing one day and a minute later, something else? I knew all along Mom wasn't on a plane, he said. I know, dummy, I know, but why'd you say it, then? Why'd you want to manipulate her and make her feel bad with all your waving at the sky? And Diego, laughing: Why didn't you tell on me? Because I felt sorry for her. Didn't it make you sad to hear her trying so hard? You just kept going with the lie. Why did you lie, Diego? You were so mean. Why *didn't* you lie, why do you always want the truth, what good is the truth? And he put on his headphones with a mocking smile. Why *do* I want the truth, Diego, when I know I'll never get it?

IT WAS EARLY SEPTEMBER when we arrived in Madrid. Diego had been really happy when his friends back home started school, but he didn't have to go. No one can hang out anymore because they're all in class, but not me. And he laughed. And our grandparents looked at him, pleased—sad, but pleased, the way they say grandparents are supposed to be: eyes tired and put-upon, but pleased, because we grandkids give them something that fulfills them. School started in August in Mexico, while in Spain it doesn't start until mid-September. We left before the fifteenth, so there was no eating pozole on Independence Day.

Soon after we got to Madrid, my mom told me I would have to work, and she took me to her friends and her friends took me to their customers and the customers took me to their children. I started to babysit some afternoons. My first employer was a Cuban woman: skinny, short, tired, with impressive boobs from so much nursing. I won't be needing you very often, because we don't have much money, but it helps when you're here, it helps me a lot. And I said yes and took care of the baby that suckled on the glass nipple and then burped on his own and settled in between my neck and shoulder and smelled like buttermilk, like all babies do. Twice a week. From four to six. And of course it made me think about Diego and remember everything we'd had to go through and how tiring it was to have to take care of him with no babysitter to help me. And then I'd turn my attention back to the baby, who breathed very quietly as if he didn't want to be a nuisance, as if he knew he was a bother to his mom, as if he felt that he'd been born without permission, like me or like Diego; that little baby, so tiny, and already feeling like an unwanted child, and yet he still had to nurse and shit and pout and look around in awe and smell me and realize that I wasn't the usual smell, but he didn't complain and I walked him around for two hours straight without ever putting him in the crib, because better quiet than crying. I didn't like to see children crying; not him, not the others I took care of. I remember that one well, because the two of us would watch his mom from the balcony. He was always quiet there behind the curtain, and I'd say: Look, there's your mommy, she's tired, she has to get away from you, and the mom would sit out there with her phone on the bench on the corner, and two or three minutes before the two hours were up she'd come back in and ask how it had gone, how the baby was, and she'd tell me her boobs were hurting and she'd be getting ready to attach the electric pump as she handed me money from her purse and thanked me and said she'd let me know the next time she needed me. And she only let me know a few times, because, Jimena told us, she was alone and had no friends and her husband didn't want to pay for a babysitter anymore, and in the end she wanted to go back home to her parents and her husband beat her and things went downhill from there, because, since she was a foreigner, no one in the building wanted to help her, and since she was one of those Cubans who spoke really loud, she wouldn't stop yelling about how that man had beaten her and how her baby was upstairs all alone and they had to help her. But the baby stayed and she went away. Why did she leave—do all mothers leave? I asked, but Jimena laughed in cahoots with my mom and told me: Girl, you think we want to leave, just because? I'd like to see you have all that trauma and baggage and still say: Oh, it's better to stay put and get caught and killed right here. And she and my mom laughed, and I didn't understand their laughter, which sounded thunderous, aggressive, harsh. But honey, let's not forget that you left too, my mom would say, and she mimicked and mocked me, and they both laughed again, and I got all kinds of pissed off, and Diego, over in a corner with his headphones on, wasn't listening, he was just gazing out the window at the sky. As if he never wanted to know a thing about our world.

I WALKED DIEGO to school on his first day. Don't be nervous, just act normal, you won't be the only one. And my eyes flitted around to show him all the heads with black hair and brown skin and features that came from the same place as us. You're going to make friends, isn't that right? And Diego, as if his feet were waterlogged, walked slowly, lazily, and said only: Uh-huh. And when I couldn't go any further with him, I told him to go ahead alone and he said: See you tomorrow, and I said: Tomorrow? And we both burst out laughing, and he was still laughing as he walked away. The first day of school he went laughing.

You and your sister, always laughing, aren't you, kiddo? my mom said to Diego when we came in together for dinner. Both of us so loud, trying not to laugh too hard, but still, his laugh was too loud, too scandalous. Scandalous? Yes, scandalous! And Diego's laugh was music—clumsy music, but music nonetheless, because it really did seem like he had an echo chamber inside his chest that made his laugh reverberate. Tremendous reverb, as if he had a whole world living inside him, one with volcanos, or mines, or whatever it was that made his laughter so cavernous and imposing. Your brother is like one of those big, loud, heavy instruments. Like a drum kit? No, those things that look like violins, but they're really big and you can't even see the people playing them. You know the ones I'm talking about? They make a deep, rich sound. I don't know what you mean, I'd say, and Diego, all laughing: Quit talking about me, I'm right here.

Diego, remember how on the first day of school you said, See you tomorrow! And Mom, who'd heard the story a hundred times, asked me again: What did he do? tell me, what did he do? And Diego laughed, covering his mouth, and I laughed too and told her about how at the school entrance he was all clingy and dreamy and so nervous and he said, See you tomorrow, and then we were laughing again. Who knows why we laughed so much over that simple thing. But we laughed a lot, the three of us. And what did your sister do then? And Diego shrugged and said he didn't know: How should I know, I was nervous. And we kept laughing, as if we'd heard the best joke in the world and survived it. Few people rise above the jokes, few have the skill to tell them, but we were a joke that laughed at itself. I felt like we were winning twice over and that's why I laughed even harder, but Diego's laughter was louder than anyone's, it was truly scandalous.

NEITHER DIEGO NOR I liked Madrid. It wasn't what we expected: it was cold and hot at the same time. Like Mexico, but colder and hotter. We didn't like how most of the neighborhoods had so many buildings so close together, so cramped and so tall, like cages, like jails, so monotonous, as though standardizing us, as though telling us we were so poor that we couldn't even have color. Plus, we had to live on the north side, and we were too lazy to go downtown. But there are so many museums, there's so much to do! Mom would say, though she had never liked museums, never liked doing anything. I don't feel like going downtown, Diego would say. Neither do I, no one does, I agreed; I don't like taking the metro. What *do* you like? Tacos, but there are no tacos here. Yes there are, downtown. I'm not going downtown for a pinche goddamn taco. Oh, you kids, Jimena told us, when I was your age I never wanted to stay inside. Neither do we, we said in unison, but we don't feel like going downtown. There's nothing there. How can there be nothing? Well, there are things, just nothing we're interested in. But there's plenty of stuff, and the same lecture over and over, but no one ever went. Not Mom, not Jimena, not Diego, not me. None of us went downtown.

Neither Diego nor I liked to take the metro, because of this one time, back in Mexico, when we got it into our heads to go all by ourselves to the station by our grandparents' house, and on the way there a man started talking dirty to me, and Diego, who was a kid but would already cuss a blue streak at anyone: I'm gonna break your fucking face in, motherfucker, he'd shouted at the man that day, and then he picked up a rock or something from the ground and threw it. It didn't hurt the man, but it grazed his body and we got scared and both of us started running and we went into the station because we thought he was chasing us. We never knew if he really was or not, but we went inside, and just like that, we jumped on a train and it took us far away. We got lost. We didn't know how to get back. We wandered a good while around stations hoping we'd recognize the one by our house, and it took us forever and our grandparents grounded us. That's why we didn't like the metro, not in Mexico and not in Madrid. We felt like it was a place with no way out, suffocating, like Madrid itself.

Yes, suffocated in Madrid, because Mom had spent years telling us how we were going to reach the promised land, and then we got there and she couldn't keep up that lie: there was no promise, no comfort, nothing; if anything, I felt a little poorer in Madrid than in Mexico; if anything, more backward and more excluded. Sure, in Mexico you could say we were poor, and we were, but at least we had company; in Madrid, people still looked at us like we were poor, but also like we were scum. Separate from them. They're not from here, they're panchitos, wetbacks, illegals. Where are you from, Bolivia? No, Mexico. And they'd start speaking Mexican to us: Oh, órale, cuate, órale güey. Where are you from, Colombia? No, Mexico. Oh, Chavo del Ocho; oh, right, tacos; oh right, spicy food. Where are you from? the employee of the Reina Sofía museum store once asked me, when we finally listened to Mom and went downtown: I'm from the Pilar neighborhood, in Madrid, I replied. She was confused and I felt victorious. I'm from where I live, I thought.

I'm from here, I live here. Do I ask other people where they come from? I complained to my mom. But she didn't get it: You two whine about everything, it's always 'no' with you two. So you like how you make a living, Mom? And just how do I make a living, what's wrong with it? And there was nothing wrong with it, but I didn't like that instead of taking care of us, our mom spent six days a week, almost eighteen hours a day, caring for a woman who looked down on her. She doesn't look down on me, what do you know? She looks at you like the Spanish parents look at Diego when he goes over to their houses. As if they had no choice but to put up with him. And my mom sighed and shook her head at me, but I knew it was true.

We also didn't like Madrid because everything was far away. The people who'd planned the metro and bus system had ensured that a three-kilometer trip would feel like six. No one could argue with me when I said that, but they still got mad. You can't talk shit about the metro to Madrileños, it's one of the things they're really proud of. They pulled the plans for that damned metro out of their asses. Anyway, my grandparents were far away too, along with the broken sidewalks and the orange juice stands on weekends and the tianguis markets and barbacoa and salsas and sweets and snow cones. It's fucking food! Mom would say when we refused to eat frozen croquettes or fish or pork. I don't like pork! Diego always said, and he didn't want to eat it, but his body, so tall and strong and teenaged, always got the better of him. You don't like pork, but you sure do eat it, my mom would say, fed up with us. You two don't like anything, you don't want anything! And it was true we didn't want any of it: we were like two little kids throwing a tantrum because we didn't like this life, because we didn't want to adapt, because we weren't allowed to adapt.

Wetback! a big, tall man once said to me in the street, and he spat at me, and I got so mad I faced him down and said: Chinga tu madre and fuck you, motherfucker, and I kept on walking, confidently, while he walked behind me and laughed, because we were both going at almost the same speed and in the same direction. I played it tough and gave him a mean look, almost haughty, almost confrontational, until he kept going straight and I turned toward the street where I lived. And I stayed hopping mad, muttering fucker, fucker, fucker really quiet, and I went up the stairs and into the kitchen and poured some water and downed it all with that attitude I got when I was on edge, all defensive and irritable, and then Diego came in and asked what was up, and I shrugged and kept drinking water, and he could tell that I was speechless with rage, and he asked again what was up, and I waved a hand to say it's nothing, but he insisted, asking if something had happened with the baby I'd gone to take care of, and I left the glass in the sink and looked him in the eyes still feeling the full force of my speechlessness and blurted: Some jerk in the street called me a wetback and spat on the ground where I was walking. Then I let out the breath I was holding in and started to cry. But you *are* a wetback, we *are* immigrants! Diego said as he hugged me, and I said yes, I was, and I went on crying in his arms, which were no longer those of a child.

U NLIKE US, Mom seemed to be in her element, as though Madrid gave her life, as though she'd been in hibernation the whole time she lived in Mexico, and a brand-new woman had emerged in Spain. And at first I hadn't understood, because in Mexico she'd been taken care of, first by my grandfather, and then her husband, and then her father again, and she always had a house and food and a mother who cared for her and siblings who, though they humiliated and teased her, were still right there, looking out for her. She didn't have anyone in Spain, or just Jimena. No friends, hardly any days off; and yet she seemed unencumbered, in spite of that little body of hers, and how bony her arms were, that little whistle she had for a voice. She seemed sure of herself. Why? Why do you like Madrid so much? It's like I don't even know you. And she looked at me and started in on her soliloquy: Well, because here I'm me, and you're you, and we don't have to answer to anybody. Here I'm so far away from everything, it's like I don't even exist there anymore. But you don't exist here, either, I said. What does it mean to be a nobody here? she asked, mocking me. It means that here people just see you as a caretaker, not as a person. And what was I in Mexico? she asked. Certainly not a caretaker! I retorted. Oh, here we go again, about how you had to do everything for Diego and my parents. Oh, you've had such a terrible childhood! What did you ever want for in Mexico? she insisted, as if we were speaking two different languages. You just don't get it at all, I replied, annoyed, because it was impossible to have a conversation with her that didn't end in a screaming match. No, we didn't get each other: she didn't get me, I didn't get her, or Madrid, and Madrid didn't get me, and none of us got Diego.

THE FIRST TIME Diego came home from school in tears, I was around because my babysitting job had canceled. He came in sobbing with rage. He slammed the front door and stormed into his room and I heard him throwing things around. What are you doing? And him: Nothing. I told him not to throw things, to be quiet, what's wrong, don't be rude, that's not how we raised you. I said all of that because I didn't want to ask What did they do to you? even though I wanted to know what they'd done; it was better to just keep scolding him. Those motherfucking culero assholes! What happened? I finally asked. And he told me kids at school had stolen his Language book, that he'd seen them do it and had gone to the guidance counselor to complain, but the guidance counselor told him he couldn't just accuse people like that, and Diego said no, he'd seen them do it and the counselor should check their backpacks, his book would be there, and the counselor said no, they weren't going to check anything. Who told you they have it? I *saw* them! And what had you done to them? I didn't do anything! And the counselor said he would deal with it, but he dealt with nothing and he didn't listen to Diego and in the classroom those brats went right on laughing at him. I could just beat the shit out of those fucking dickheads, he told me, trembling and clenching a fist. And I nodded and said yes, he *could* do that, but he wasn't going to. Why not? Wimpy little shits. For the same reason your guidance counselor wouldn't listen to you, and Diego pressed his lips together and nodded. Fucking culeros, pinches assholes, he said, and I promised I would buy him a new copy of the book, and he said no, he would get it back from them, and I insisted that we would buy the book so he could get over this, and he refused, wanting to fight back, but I made him, and I took the forty euros I had earned those days watching other people's kids at two different houses, and I bought my brother the Language book that cost 33.40, so he could go on listening to his music in the small, dark room where he lived, without having to think about what was going on outside. So Diego could go on being Diego.

I T WASN'T REALLY ABOUT SCHOOL. I'd felt far removed from school for a long time myself, back in Mexico, knowing that someday I'd be leaving and anything I built there would be worthless. I stopped paying attention, stopped trying. But it was different with Diego. I wanted him to study no matter what it took. Study, Diego, don't get paralyzed by that fear, because I see fear in you when you don't study. You can do it, you know you can! And Diego said no, he didn't want to study, as soon as he finished high school he'd say to hell with it all. And what are you going to do then? I'll figure it out. Don't be dumb, Mom didn't bust her ass just so you could say shit like that. *You* study, then, he'd say, and I'd tell him to shut up. *You* study, dumbass, he said, and he'd put on his headphones and leave me there talking to myself, because it wasn't about school, it was about Diego and the desperation I felt seeing him turn into this tornado of useless ideas, because I could sense the red-hot rage in his eyes and in his walk and in the noise he made when he sighed; I could sense the volcano inside him. Study, Diego, I said it so many times, but he'd just turn up his music louder and louder so he couldn't hear.

T HE FIRST TIME Diego got into a fight at school they called home, but neither Mom nor I answered the phone. I didn't hear it ring. We went on with our day, even had dinner in the kitchen, exchanged our schedules for the week and decided who would cook what on which days. I was washing the Tupperware my mom took to work with her because they didn't feed her at that house—she could eat when the old lady took a nap, but often didn't have time to wash the containers because there was always some emergency. Then Diego came into the kitchen and saw I was there and avoided meeting my eyes. You can at least say hi, right? But he opened the freezer and took out some ice and started to walk away. What's the ice for? And clear as day I saw the expression on his face that said, Fuck, she's on to me. What are you drinking? I asked. But Diego wasn't drinking anything, he had a small but stubborn cut on his cheek and it wouldn't close. Fuck, what the hell, Diego! and Diego telling me to shut up. We went to his room and he told me that he'd beaten up three guys, just him all by himself, but between the three of them they'd gotten in some hits too. I won, obviously, but the fuckers did land a few punches. But why, Diego, why?! And then he was saying I wouldn't understand. Explain it to me! and he said no, and I said yes, yes, I needed to know. And he wouldn't explain, but said I'd have to sign the report they'd sent home with him; and I said no, not until he gave me an explanation. I can sign it myself, I've done it lots of times before, but I wanted to tell you, he said, irritated. And what did they say at school? Nothing really, they didn't care that much, they just suspended me. They called the house and your cell phones, but you and Mom didn't answer, he said, as though pointing the finger at us, and then I checked and it was true, I did have three missed calls. But what happened? Nothing happened: fucking culero assholes, I just got fucking sick of them, that's all. And then? Then, nothing, just sign it, because I want to do things right. Right means not hitting people, Diego. Goddammit, sign it and support me. Stand up for me, I didn't do anything, god-fucking-dammit, I didn't do anything! And it was the way he said that, the way his eyes looked at me as his lip trembled with frustration, that made me sign the paper and help him so the ice wouldn't hurt. I put a little Band-Aid on his wound so it would close overnight.

Scoot over, I'll hang here with you for a while. You want to listen to music, or talk? Music, he said, and we put on Vampire Weekend, the upbeat album, the one that made us feel happy, the one that made us dance on Saturdays while we scrubbed the floor and washed clothes. Play that one, he told me, and we put it on and sang along together, our voices low so Mom wouldn't hear. And several times we even drummed our fingers like we were dancing, and when I saw he was starting to fall asleep, I left him alone and turned out the light and said good night. Should I leave the music on? And he said yes, start it over again. And I started the album from the first song and turned down the volume and let him sleep.

Then I went to say goodnight to my mom, and casually asked if she'd had any missed calls, and she shot me a bored look as she massaged lotion into her feet. No one ever calls me. You're sure? I asked again. Sure, she said, and I stayed a couple seconds longer to see if she would move to check her phone, but she didn't say anything else and I said see you tomorrow and she told me to close the door behind me and to knock next time before barging in.

THAT LAST SUMMER IN MEXICO, Mom promised that she would come get us in December, in time for Christmas. Even I got excited and promised Diego that this time we really were going to cook dinner in the oven, he and I, and that we would go see the planes from close up and we'd watch as Mom disembarked and Diego was all, Yeah, of course we will, and I heard him telling his friends that his mom was really coming for him and at Christmas we would all be together and that he was even going to invite his grandparents, his dad's parents, because enough already with the Christmases without Mom, and how she'd be bringing him lots of presents and who cared if she didn't live with us right now, our mom was going to come for us and we would never be apart again. But Mom dropped the ball, and in November when we asked when she was coming in she said, Oh no, that she'd forgotten and had already put her savings into the bank to be ready next year, yes, next year she would come for us.

Even with all that disappointment, I asked my grandmother to buy some chicken and to bring home pineapples and cherries and I volunteered to cook some recipes I'd found online, and said that, instead of turkey, I'd make some very good grilled chicken with all the fixings, potatoes and sauces, and my grandmother said ok; and we planned a party for Diego and made him help us clean; and my aunts and uncles came with their own dishes, but

Diego insisted that our mom was coming, he thought that was the real surprise, that when we least expected it, as a Christmas Eve gift, she was going to ring the doorbell and he would go let her in. My chicken came out bland and sickly sweet and inedible, and even so my grandmother put it on the table and praised it and my aunts and their kids said how pretty it was, that Diego should try some and that I had a real knack for cooking, and there I was with my stomach churning, sad, angry, *really* angry, thinking about my mother's lies and about how bad the chicken tasted and all I wanted was to crawl under the table, but I just smiled and my grandfather served himself a leg and potatoes and pineapple and I could tell he was struggling to eat it, but he ate, and there we were, in the middle of my aunts' laughter and conversation, my grandparents and me, trying to mask my mom's absence. But then she called, and my grandmother softened; she always softened up to my mother's sporadic gestures of love, and she called out excitedly to Diego: It's your mom! And Diego, with his brow furrowed and his mouth in a pout, said he didn't want to talk, and Abuela was all, Yes, come on now, talk to her, and Diego went to the table and sat down and asked me to serve him some chicken, and Abuela was like, Go on, answer, and Diego only said, Give me some more, and Abuelo and I were cutting more chicken breast for Diego, and when Diego had his plate he looked at us furiously and squeezed the meat in his fingers and threw the pieces at our grandmother and went to his room and screamed that he didn't want to hear it, that he wasn't going to talk to Mom until she came for him. And he locked the door and wouldn't let us in and we told him to open up and he started to hit the door and make guttural sounds, grum, grooom, gruuum, in a full-on tantrum. And that's why our mother came for us at the end of August and took us to Madrid.

C AN YOU SING if you're an airplane pilot? Can you listen to music in a plane while you're flying through the clouds? I don't think so, Diego, you have to pay attention to instructions from the control tower. What if I sing to myself, or hum? Oh, well, maybe you could hum, sure, but real quiet, though it'll be hard for you with that loud-ass voice of yours, you'll have a tough time singing to yourself. And then I'll feel like singing really loud, like I'm yelling, but yeah, it's true that my voice is really big, he said. And that's why you don't sing? I sing in my mind, and then I read along online with the songs I listen to, and I sing with my eyes. Oh, sure, with your eyes, dumbass! Hey, asshole! So, what do you sing? I sing all kinds of stuff, but a lot of Vampire, of course. Well, you go ahead and sing, what are they going to say? Nobody will understand any of it. And it's not like the neighbors are going to try and shut you up. Sometimes when I'm mad I want to sing, do you ever feel like that? he asked. Yeah, sometimes, I said. And then I want to scream but it's better to sing, and I sing a lot, but I don't know why I'm mad. I feel like I have a hole here in my stomach, he said, pointing to his belly, and like something really hot is rising up here, and he touched his chest and then his throat, and the only thing that calms me down is to scream. Do you ever get that feeling? Yeah, sometimes. And what do you do? Well, I sing, too, when there's no one around, when you're at school and Mom's not home. I sing real quiet, but with the music up loud. The thing is that I'm hardly ever alone, he said. Well, you go ahead and sing, you're always noisy anyway. Like this? and he started to pretend he was singing like a soprano, like in the opera, and we laughed. I really thought pilots could sing, or I wanted to believe they could: just imagine, singing while you fly, it must be really cool, he told me, returning to his serious tone, the usual one. Yeah, it must be cool. Do you think we'll ever get used to Madrid? Sure, I think so. I hope so, he said, I hope so, because I don't want to live like this, but I don't want to die.

I WAS LIVING in Barcelona when Diego jumped from the fifth floor. I'd been living there for a while. When I got the call I was lying in bed, half asleep, and at first it was like a dream: the buzz of the phone made me think it was one of those cocky mosquitoes that come around at my grandmother's house in summer. The kind that even if you shoo them away will get under your clothes, bite you something fierce, leave you with a red welt. The kind that stay cocky even if you turn on a light and throw a sandal at them: I *will* bite you, and then they do. That was how the phone was: one, two, three, four, five times buzzing at me until I woke up and saw that I wasn't in Mexico, but in Barcelona.

He's dead, he's dead, Mom told me when I got ahold of her, and I was speechless, thinking how I would have preferred a million red welts to what I was hearing. I hung up as soon as I could and sat staring at the wall, remembering all we had gone through in Madrid after we'd arrived: both of us desperate and seeing enemies everywhere, but too afraid to kill. Then I bought my train ticket to Madrid; I had to get there fast but I wanted to delay my arrival, so I went to the beach instead of the station. On the bus there, the word "Mom" appeared incessantly on my phone screen, silent, just a single chime with that word that came and went over and over, and I looked at it as if my mother were trapped in a time and place I couldn't reach, and instead

I put the phone away, and though it vibrated and I felt it on my elbow, I didn't answer, shooing more imaginary bugs away.

I spent a long time looking out at the sea, playing with the sand like Diego had when he was six years old and we took him to the park and he ran straight to the sandbox and Abuelo and I told him that the sandbox was for little kids and Diego promised he wouldn't bother anyone but would we please let him play, and he played. And it was as if I had Diego there in front of me with the cold ocean that kept trying to splash my feet and I wouldn't let it. What did you want to say, Diego, that I wouldn't listen to? And his little baby body, with his black black hair and his dark dark skin, like that of the men who walked among the beach towels and asked if we wanted beer, and most people didn't answer but grabbed hold of their things out of fear that the men would rob them. That's how Diego was, among us all, making noise, calling our attention only to disappear from sight. Like that, that's what he was like, my Diego, his little body covered in sand and his shoes dirty and me angry because I was the one who would have to wash them, I would have to wash his feet. That's how Diego was, no photographer there to capture his pain, no image of him that would circle the world and win prizes. No one there with Diego. My brother's body alone, no echo, no slogans, because who cared about one more kid from a random neighborhood in Madrid, yet another kid who hadn't even been born there. Diego, like that, all alone, with two or three curious onlookers dying of hunger and hope just like him; just like that, Diego, no ocean in the background, no sand, or Instagram, no artists or juries saying his death was symbolic. Just like that, all alone, no one there to tell him not to do it. No one with Diego, and his pain winning out over his will. No one with his blood on the asphalt, not even the goddamn mosquitoes.

PART TWO

I WAITED AT Passeig de Sant Joan until lunchtime. We'd agreed to meet at eleven thirty, but the woman looking for a nanny for her kids never showed up to interview me. I was starving, but I still hadn't gotten used to paying almost four euros for a breakfast of coffee and bread with tomato. I felt very alone. This was the third time I'd been referred by people who were supposedly Martina's close friends, people who promised me a job and didn't come through. I didn't have much money. I was homesick, but I didn't want to go back to Madrid. I walked until I reached the corner by Casa Batlló. I liked the building, and although the hordes of tourists blocked my view of the entrance, I was content to look up at the windows. I sent a second message to Martina and collided with a couple of starry-eyed guys who wouldn't let go of each other's hands long enough to get their tickets. As if from over six feet up they couldn't even see little me. Or precisely because they had, they felt no qualms about ignoring me. Fuckers, I thought. Assholes. The only other option is to work in-house, Martina's return message said. It never rains but it pours, I thought. The problems come all at once, like they want to compete to see which one will finally make us really lose it. A few stairs, a little piece of rug, and I stumbled again, this time into a group of women walking out in both directions, taking up the whole sidewalk like it was a big city block. I pretended to get in line to buy tickets to the museum so I wouldn't look so clumsy, so out of place. I said yes to Martina. I agreed to work in-house for four hundred fifty euros a month. Under the table, Martina said. Sundays are yours, and consider yourself lucky, because that's a luxury. I swallowed hard. I said ok. The cloudy sky, almost grayish white, started pouring rain. I left the museum line and walked to the metro station. What I most remember about Barcelona is the white sky of that day.

TWO WEEKS INTO my job as a live-in caretaker, I already wanted to quit. I wasn't even alone when I slept. I shared a room with the woman I was caring for. She snored and smelled bad. It didn't matter how much I washed her skin, her hair, her mouth. Turned out it was the mattress protector that was so rank I felt like throwing up. I figured it out after I'd made sure to wash the sheets, blankets, comforter. Also the floor, with bleach, and the furniture with scented cleaner, and the lamps, old and yellowed but valuable, *molt valuoses*, which the woman's daughter wouldn't throw out even though they didn't turn on anymore. You have no idea how much it costs to maintain this house, everything here is valuable, she told me, and I nodded. Yes, yes, but what about that rancid smell? It took me almost a week to find its source. Keep everything neat, as if you weren't even here, it's important to her, the daughter told me. And I nodded: as if I weren't even here. But the smell came back, it was unbearable, it had more of a presence than I did.

You're going to go to the beach, huh? the daughter asked. Yes, I said. You'll like it, but don't go to Barceloneta, it's all tourists there. None of the Barcelona beaches are any good. You should go to Badalona, at least, there are people from your country there, and there's a Mexican restaurant on the main avenue. You know how to get to Badalona? I shook my head. Well, whatever. Go wherever you want, she told me, and then she gave me the paper with the week's to-do list: the prescription, the medicine for her mother, the days, hours, the menu, her own clothes, her boyfriend's, her mother's. Everything engineered in a quasi-perfect schedule that accounted for every hour I lived in that place. And have you thought about what you'll do over the holidays? You're not going to your country to see your family, right? I smiled. My family lives in Madrid. Will you go there? Because you should know that when we hired you, we thought you would stay here. We want to go to the Alps. Will you stay? You should know that it's this kind of thing that we need you for. The whole vacation? I asked. Yes, well, the important days, I know, we should have stipulated this before we hired you. These are the things that we need you for. Well, I don't know, I said. I'll have to talk to my family about it. The daughter's boyfriend chimed in: *Et vaig dir que havies de ser una dona que visqués sola al país, no te'n pots refiar.* The daughter made an annoyed face. Think about it while you're at the beach, we'll give you an extra fifty euros for the month if you stay over the holidays! I nodded while I picked up my backpack and phone and left, feeling both of them staring at the back of my neck.

I didn't want to go to Madrid, but neither did I want that family to feel like they owned me. Fifty euros? Jimena asked. Girl, tell her to stick those fifty euros up her ass and come spend the holidays with your brother, the kid gets more unbearable by the day! What did he do now? I asked, not really wanting to know. Oh, honey, I won't even tell you, you won't believe your ears! But should I say no right away? I asked. I don't want them giving me dirty looks all the time. What if I send them a message tomorrow when they're not right in front of me? I asked. Wait for the holidays and then fuck 'em! she said, very sure of herself. Go have a beer and then decide. I said ok and hung up.

I HADN'T SPOKEN to my mother since I'd left Madrid. You're doing the same thing to me that I did to my parents. Traitor! And emojis of smiles and laughter. My mother, always laughing at me. Always needling me, making out that my reactions to her were childish, immature, silly, and excessive—above all excessive. The day I left, I shoved her. She tried to take my keys away and I went at her, threw her back onto her bed and ran to my room. I don't think she ever expected me to push her. But I wanted to leave. I couldn't take it anymore. I grabbed a few things and left the house. Later I called Jimena and she helped me get to Barcelona. You're making a mistake, because you'll never be better off than at your mother's house! But I told her I was never going back. And she sent me to Martina.

Martina was a Bolivian woman, married to a man who was Argentine-Spanish. They lived on Consell de Cent, near Tetuán. I went to stay at their house. She came to pick me up at the train station. She fed me, because she was a good friend of Jimena's. We've been through a lot together, Martina told me. I met Jimena when she first got here and was still scared of her mom, who stabbed her after she came out as a lesbian—that's why she moved to Spain. If Jimena vouches for you, you're welcome here. But get to work—everyone works in this house. Martina lived with her husband, her eight-month-old baby, and two of her nieces. All the women were Bolivian. All of them had more kids back in La Paz and Cochabamba. All were sending money to their families and looking for ways to bring their kids to Barcelona. They were all also trying to avoid working as live-in help. Working in-house is the worst, but it's what you can always find, they told me. That's why I didn't want to do it. Sometimes they ration your food and you go hungry, the nieces went on. They always look down on you; even when they smile, they're looking down on you. They call you panchita, right? I asked once, wanting to contribute to the conversation. And the two nieces laughed. Oh, just ignore them. You do your thing. And they did their thing— Ainara and Olga had their work permits and held down jobs at several hotels in Barcelona. But even with of all their contacts, no one ever called me back, and I ended up in Rosselló, very close to the Sagrada Familia Basilica, taking care of the woman with the ottoman until my mother's midnight call.

THE ONLY CONTACTS I had in my phone were my grandparents, Jimena, Mom, Martina, and Diego. I didn't talk to anyone else, wasn't close enough to anyone else to justify a chat. Diego hardly ever texted me, and when he did, it was all just memes and jokes. I responded with emojis. We hadn't spoken since the night before I left home. Neither of us felt like starting a real conversation and both of us pretended it wasn't happening. It *was* happening. But I felt things were better that way, with emojis and memes, acting like teenagers who just don't know how to talk to each other. And that's what I was, except with my mom. I really wouldn't communicate with her at all, I didn't respond to her WhatsApp messages or say thank you or anything. I felt guilty and I missed her, but I thought I didn't. Just like that, far away like the sun. You have to keep your family far away but still present, like the sun, Jimena would say to me. And I did listen to what Jimena said.

That night, following our evening ritual, the woman and I were getting ready for bed; she'd eaten a little gazpacho, a little toast with olive oil, a little stewed apple. Are you finished, ma'am? Yes, I've finished. Take me to brush my teeth. And I helped her clean her teeth and put them in again. She didn't like to sleep without her dentures, even though her daughter told her it was dangerous to wear them. Then I'd brush her hair in front of the mirror and ask her to go pee. Let's go pee, ma'am! And she always said ok, and I sat her down and then cleaned her with a damp wipe, and she told me not to look. Don't look at me, please, don't look at me. And I'd say that I wasn't looking and I put my face right in front of hers and said: I can't see you, look, my eyes are closed, and she leaned against me while I maneuvered to wipe her clean. But that night the woman said: I don't want you looking at me anymore, don't look anymore. Leave. Get out of this bathroom. Leave me alone, I know what I'm doing, I'll do it myself. And we argued a bit, I said no, she said yes, until I surrendered and gave her a little dignity and let her urinate alone. Afterward, though, she did have me wash her hands and braid her hair for bed and dress her in a clean nightgown.

Give me the white nightgown from the wardrobe, here's the key, get my white nightgown. And she took the key from her nightstand and I opened her wardrobe and took out the white nightgown and helped her put it on. My husband gave me this nightgown, and I used to wear it every Friday when we came back from the beach and showered and listened to the radio in the parlor. Have you seen my parlor and all the paintings? They're all originals. All by childhood friends of mine. All of them from here. And have you seen the ottoman I have in the parlor? You have beautiful furniture, ma'am, I told her as she tried to stand up. Have you seen how lovely the portraits are? The one in the hallway is of my brother. He worked for the Catalan government. And I got to keep it. He gave me the ottoman, too. Have you seen those things yet? Yes, of course I've seen them. I had women working here, taking care of me when I was little, just like you do now. But they were Andalusian, you know? Where are you from? I'm from Mexico, ma'am. Oh, we just love Mexico! The songs. The mariachis. Isn't that right? Yes, ma'am. Come lie down, it's late and your daughter is coming tomorrow. Come, it's bedtime,

I told her. And her, stubborn: But I haven't shown you the ottoman! And she got up and I followed her to the parlor where the
ottoman was and she sat down on an armchair and said: look at
that fabric, it's antique, from the eighteenth century. Just like at
the Royal Palace. Look, and she reached out her hand and I took
it and she moved to sit on the ottoman and then both of us, at
the same time, in the same second, looked at each other, because
the lady was peeing herself. Ma'am, no! And then the urine was
pooling and soaking into the whole ottoman and the lady was
trying to throw herself to the floor and she was calling me an
idiot, a brute. Furious, she groped around on the wet floor while
I tried to get her up and she screamed at me to leave her alone,
to let her be. Leave me alone, you stupid, useless squaw! And I
let go of her and let her get all wet while she went on insulting
me and I wrote a message to Jimena trying to explain what had
happened. You peasant, you wetback, you greaser! she shouted.
You've ruined all my furniture, get out of here, get out! And she
went on yelling every insult she could think of, and I wanted to
run away, I didn't know what to do, until my mom called me,
right at midnight, and told me: Get out of there, get out of there.
And I was crying and hardly able to contain myself and I said ok
and wiped my nose, I said ok and she repeated: Get out of there
and don't take another euro from them. Tomorrow I'll transfer
money to hold you over until you find another job. And me, crying, saying ok and getting the bucket to clean the floor and the
ottoman and running a bath for the lady who, two minutes later,
was asking me in a quiet voice to bathe her and brush her hair
and give her something to eat. I did it all, and the woman let me
do it, saying, Softer, do it softer, and I treated her more softly, but
I couldn't be any softer after that, because inside I didn't care at
all about that ottoman, and I didn't care if she called me a squaw,

but it did hurt me that I had to shut up and serve her, as if just minutes before she hadn't been slapping at me and calling me names. It was very softly then that I got her back into bed and cleaned the floor and took the ottoman out to the balcony to get rid of the urine stench. Then I sent a message to her daughter saying that this was my last night, and she read the message, but didn't answer. The next day, at nine in the morning, I left the building with my backpack and nothing else. Before closing the door behind me, the daughter's boyfriend told me: Panchita, you should go back to your own country. That was the only time he ever spoke to me in Spanish and not Catalan.

OLGA WAS THE ONE who cried the most over being so far away from her children. She had three. With two different fathers, neither of whom took responsibility for their kids. She was a young, single mother. She couldn't find work in Bolivia, and since her aunt Martina could find it in Spain, she took her advice and asked their whole family for money so she could buy a ticket there. It wasn't easy, Olga told me. They ask for a lot of papers, and we couldn't get them all. It took me five years to get a Foreigner Identity Number. What about your kids? I asked. They stayed back home, with my mom and my sister. I just paid off the debt with my family last year, but kids grow up and they ask for things, you know? Yeah, I said. And I thought about my mom and all those years that she was surely also paying off her debt and sending us money because we asked for things. It's the littlest one that hurts the most, I didn't even get to nurse him. He was two months old when I came here. What could I do? We were starving to death and everyone looked down on me because I had kids and no one was supporting me. I'm sorry, I said. Don't be sorry, she replied, mad at herself for saying "We were starving to death." We weren't starving, you know? It was just that I didn't want a life like that, and I saw how Martina's kids came back from their visits with money and good clothes and they could go out and buy things, and I wanted that for my kids, you know? Yes, I know. Sorry, I was just thinking about my own mom, I told her. And so I came here, she said, and look, don't say anything to Martina, but I'm joining up with a sort of union. There are a bunch of us who want to change the way we're treated. We're organizing. Your cousin, too? I asked. No, not Ainara. She says Martina will get mad, that she'll yell at us. But you know what? It's all good with Martina until it's not. Seriously, you'll see. She talks all nice until the Martina in her goes to her head and then everything is all wrong, and I know she's not going to like this unionizing thing, but whatever, you know? You can come too, anytime you want.

And I went, because I still couldn't find anything but live-in work. In the meantime, Martina had integrated me into a system that she kept pretty tightly controlled: she rented houses and then re-rented them to several other people. She also offered a cleaning service for those houses that she provided herself, and whenever she had too many houses to clean, she sent me or Ainara or whoever else. But generally she did it herself, so I was lucky if I cleaned two houses a week and ended up with forty euros, which I then had to give back to Martina to pay for the room I shared with Olga and contribute to food for us all. And I understood that's how things were, but I didn't want to depend on her. Why do you go to those union meetings with Olga, when you don't even have a job? Ainara asked me. But I felt like I needed to go just because staying where I was, living in someone else's house, was driving me nuts.

You should come back to Madrid, Jimena insisted, but I needed to prove to my mom that I could fend for myself, that we could have another kind of relationship where she wasn't the one in charge, the one who decided for me. Well, screw you then, my mom told me. Screw you, screw you. And I thought: Yep,

I'm screwed, all by myself, without you. Until that night when she told me to get out of that house and she sent me money. I'm not screwing up on my own, I thought, we're screwing me up together. I'm screwing her over, screwing myself over. But I'm not going back to Madrid.

I also went to those union meetings so I could get in with the cousins. The cousins? Yes, because in order to get jobs, one by one, we would recommend each other as cousins. She's really good and so hard-working—plus she's my cousin! And when you said that to the bosses, their attitude changed. Well, if she's your cousin, bring her in, she can be your responsibility. And it didn't matter if they were Ecuadorean, Dominican, or Bolivian, they were all cousins. As long as they know Spanish, it's all good, we're not setting up a refugee camp here, is what the hotel bosses apparently said. And it was hard to become a cousin, because the cousins all had official work permits. No one can threaten to report us now, and we can make demands. What demands? Well, for all our rights. The overtime they don't pay us because they say we're slow. And where they used to assign us ten rooms to clean, now it's double. Not enough time in the world. And what about health problems? Well, yes, all of them: one had a bad back, another arthritis. And nothing, no sick leave or anything. We have to keep working, or else other cousins will come. There are always more cousins, you know? Olga said. Yes, I know. There will never be a lack of cousins, and instead of that being used against us, what we want is to really be like cousins, you know? To help each other, for people to respect our rights. Yes, *their* rights. What rights did I have? None, since I didn't even have a job. Someday you'll be a cousin, you just wait, you'll see. And so I started going to the meetings every Wednesday at six P.M.

I MET CARLOTA AND MANUELA at the cousins' meetings. Every Wednesday, after the meeting, Carlota and Manuela went dancing at a Cuban bar. I started going with them. I felt like they were my friends. Mom, zero; me, one. I was winning. It was the first time I'd had people around me since I'd come to Spain. And I was learning a lot. They were the ones who told me that if I wanted to stay in Barcelona, I had to learn Catalan. Without Catalan you're nothing. You are nothing, ever, but without Catalan, you're even less. Hook up with a Catalan guy, it's faster, they told me, and they started a Tinder account for me. But on Tinder I matched with Gastón. One date. Argentine, very full of himself. Not at all interesting. Mexican? Che, you're a goddess, he told me. Screw that. He was boring, tactless, phony. I didn't see him again and I deleted Tinder.

Once I'd gotten started with Catalan, I signed up for English classes too, at a center close to Passeig de Sant Joan. It was a language institute that gave certificates to aspiring English teachers, and because it was summer they had almost no students to practice on, so they offered free classes. I went, even though Martina said, Less study and more work. I *am* working, I told her, and I paid the forty euros a week she charged me. Mom transferred eighty a week into my account. I ate badly, slept badly, but I thought learning English and Catalan would help me more than cleaning bathrooms would. This one wants to be all international, Carlota and Manuela would say. And we'd laugh, but still I kept on going to the meetings to listen to them and to watch them organize, and there were always more and more cousins who wanted to make some noise.

I met Tom in English class. Scottish. Tall, thin, blond pony-tail. When I went into the classroom he was writing on the board. Then more students came in and he turned around to see us all and I thought he was cute, and he looked at me differently, too. I took six classes with him, and then he got his certification and stopped teaching there, and that was when he asked for my phone number. Want to get coffee? Yes, I said. But then it wasn't coffee, it was a walk through Ciudadela Park. Everything with him was a contradiction. His gentle, sheep-like face, looking me right in the eye while he made insulting comments about Colombia. I lived in Colombia for three years, the people are great, but they deserve what they get. It's like they have corruption in their bones. I don't think that's true, Tom, it's not like that. No, really, I was there, I know, I lived there for three years. And then he would take my hand and say things that sometimes I didn't hear because something inside me was still echoing, the discomfort of knowing that what he said was wrong but not knowing how to respond. But I'd smile at him and let him hold my hand. What's up with Carlota and Manuela? They're my cousins. Also Mexican? Yes, yes. They're Mexican too.

Tom—Tomás, to us—came dancing every Wednesday, and eventually every Saturday, too. Carlota and Manuela, who shared a house with an Italian woman who went to Girona every weekend to visit a guy she'd hooked up with, let me act like their house was mine when Tom came to pick me up on Saturdays. Then Tom took it for granted that I had a nice house and enough money to live in Barcelona and go out and have fun. You need to

think more about your future, he'd say, you can't just keep living it up like some rich kid trustifarian. I grew up in poverty, my
parents always had to ask the government for help, my brother
and I never had things handed to us. I know what it's like to live
in poverty. I don't want you to have to go through all that just
because you're not making the most of your opportunities now.
And I said yes, of course. You're right.

Why do you go to Sants on Wednesdays with your cousins? he
asked me. Our final project for our master's is going to be about
the cleaning women who work in hotels, I told him. Wow, what
about them? It's really interesting, they're organizing to demand
their rights. Wow, qué guay, tía, that's awesome! How's it going?
It's going well, they want to unionize, and they haven't been able
to do it yet, but they're trying to figure it out. There's a law student who's helping them. And then some college students are
advising them, too, it's pretty cool. And what are you all doing,
are you also advising them? No, we just listen so we can write it
up for our master's thesis. Qué guay, that's so cool! See? Try to
learn from those women, they have a lot to teach you. Yes, I said,
and I left him smiling and happy that he was showing me how to
get my life on track.

Qué guay, tía, so cool, you and your cousins, the researchers!
Carlota and Manuela laughed. You don't seem to realize that
you're going to get caught lying and then you'll regret missing out
on your only chance to marry a European. Marry a European,
miss out, I scoffed. Get married? Fuck that! And we laughed at
the advice we gave ourselves.

I had as much contempt for Tom-Tomás as I did affection.
Both things at once. Suddenly he could seem like a little kid who
was all alone and would die without ever understanding a thing.
Tía, girl, lass, let's go eat vegan food, my beauty, my darling,

vegan so we don't kill any little animals, even though the qui-
noa I'm eating is exploiting the lands of your cousins the "Mexicans." And Carlota and me, laughing. Joder, tía, he doesn't even
realize I'm Colombian, even though he lived there! cried Manuela. Honey, sweetie, we're going to separate all the recycling, so
the girl who does the cleaning can throw out all our garbage for
us. Hooooooneeeeeyyy. That fucker, that limey gonorrea who
doesn't even know how to dance, comes around here telling *us*
how to be buenas good girls. You need to learn English, honey, so
I can take you to my country without feeling embarrassed. And I
laughed, because it was all true and that was why I resented him.
But I also liked him. I liked his honey-colored eyes, and the way
his hands caressed my face when we were lying in his bed. I liked
that he made me breakfast and that he encouraged me to learn
English. That he let me sleep at his house almost every night
and that on Sundays we had picnics at the beach. Everything
was good with him, until it wasn't: he smoked too much weed,
and had shouting matches with his dad every time they talked.
He complained about working eight hours a day and said stupid
things about his students. Jackasses, almost all of them eejits,
almost all of them dickheads because they couldn't get their
accents just right, because they didn't take learning seriously.
They'll never get anywhere that way, they'll always be just what
they are. How's your thesis going? I never see you study. Oh, it's
going. And then I'd spend a few days at Martina's house or at
Carlota and Manuela's and I'd tell him I'd had a fit of inspiration.

I also liked him because we made plans: Next year we can go
to Scotland so you can meet my parents, we can spend Christmas
there. Yes, I said. When you finish your thesis and defend it, we'll
have dinner at one of those trendy Japanese restaurants you see
everywhere now, my treat. And that "my treat" seemed very nice,

because Tom never paid for anything. Nothing. He even asked me for money on the days when I stayed at his house: for tea, for bread, for juice. Hon, we have to be equals, we have to contribute the same. We didn't take the subway much either, or the bus, because he said it was bad for the environment, and sometimes we would slog four kilometers to get somewhere. Still, when we went to other people's houses or were at Carlota and Manuela's, he devoured everything in sight: You have Colombian tamales? there's salad? give me two, three plates. Gluttonous, abusive. Your freeloading Brit. He wants the milk, but not the cow. Tell him you don't have a job! Tell the truth! But I no longer knew what the truth was, and I really liked that he could respect me, and that he thought I was smart and that he massaged my feet while watching movies or caressed my hair while I read. Tell him to take the stick out of his ass and contribute, con-triii-buuute! Manuela would say. But neither Tom nor I was being honest.

THE COUSINS WERE working on a sort of communication strategy along with several college girls who felt committed to the cause. They started a blog, a Twitter account, a Facebook page. They put up news about progress and setbacks. They denounced the abuse suffered by members of the collective, and they filmed testimonial videos, always with blurred faces, of people describing the things they had endured. Rosario, from Paraguay, had one of the most serious cases: inhaling so many chemicals from cleaning products was causing health problems, and her skin was breaking out in a rash from so much bleach. She needed to quit, but if she quit there was no money, and her son was in his last year of high school, she couldn't let him down. Then Manuela and Carlota said that we all had to band together, go on strike, form alliances with other collectives. With the college girls as intermediaries, some of the cousins approached other feminist groups. Even Tom heard about it. You have to tell your classmates from the master's program to do something! My dear, this is big! I told him not to meddle. But this is really huge! But it's not your concern, Tom, don't stick your nose in. But his nose was already in. He started showing up at the meetings, and they wouldn't let him in but he stayed outside, supposedly waiting for me. Don't wait for me, I don't want you here! But he kept going, because, I don't know, he thought being there made him a revolutionary or something. Then the college girls started to turn on him: Get out of here, macho man, you're not welcome. Go away, asshole, gilipollas, we don't want you here! But I'm here to support my girlfriend! Who's your girlfriend? The master's student, she's a college girl like you! Who? asked the student with dreadlocks. The Mexican girl—there are three Mexicans, and one is my girlfriend. All three of them are master's students. And the dreadlocked girl came in with her holier-than-thou attitude and asked who the master's students were, and no one said anything. And I kept my head down and went on listening to how the March 8 protest would be organized and all the reasons why we, the immigrants, the cleaning women, the ones who took care of Spain's old people, were the ones who should lead the march. The college girls said that it might not be possible, because there were a lot of other collectives that could also demand to go first. So, there aren't any master's students here? asked the dreadlocked girl. And everyone shouted: No!

Liar, asshole, me cago en tus muertos! dreadlocks yelled at Tom as she shooed him away. He never came back to Sants, and then he started to turn on me, and he stopped inviting me to his house as much, and he joined a band that practiced on weekends. We stopped seeing so much of each other. He only calls you when he wants to fuck, Manuela said. That son of a bitch doesn't deserve you, Carlota said. Your mom's been supporting both of you for the past three months, and then the asshole goes and treats you like this, they said. They were right. But I want to fuck, too. I want to get off, too. I want it all!

How about today? he texted me out of the blue, and I said yes, but that I wasn't feeling great, could we just watch a movie. Well, another time if you want. No, I want to see you today, it's just that I'm not feeling great. But what does that mean? Are you sick? Sí, estoy sick. Just stay home then. No, I want to hang out. I want to fuck with you. Ok, come over. And I went. And we fucked, follábamos, fuckeábamos. Roughly. Always rough. As if he were incapable of a gentle touch. As if he had lost that sort of tenderness, empathy, reciprocity during sex. Just sex like teenagers, but still sex. It couldn't be any other way. But it wasn't like before, because he was still waiting for me to apologize for lying, and so he acted like a prick. Are you ever going to apologize for letting your friends humiliate me like that? And I just rolled my eyes and kept quiet, because really, what could I say? What explanation was I going to give him? You really are a pendejo, was what I wanted to say, but all I said was: I don't want to talk about it. Just like we didn't talk about anything else.

Why are you two together if you're not together? Just to fuck, said Manuela. That's how this asshole is, such a gonorrea of a prick. It makes me want to call your mom and tell her that you don't study or work, all you do is sit around and wait to see what time some guy is going to come pick you up. And why should I have to wash other people's asses? I asked. Why should I have to clean all those bathrooms for ten euros an hour? Ten!? Because that's what it pays, dumbass! she retorted. Where do you think your mom gets the money she sends you? You think she just shits it out? With everything you've gone through, plus everything with the cousins, and still it's like you're zumbá, like you're crazy! Nutso, chalada, you're crazy and I don't want you coming to our meetings anymore, because you're no help, you won't commit, you don't contribute anything and all you do is parade your little blond tourist around and have him come pick you up so you can feel all superior! Don't come back to our meetings, or to our house, or anything! And if you need a place to crash, then go ask that son of a bitch, that hueón, that fucking gilipollas of yours! Let him take you in, but you can't be here anymore, we're done! Manuela yelled at me, and I didn't know what to say and when you don't know what to say it's best to keep quiet and act offended and turn your back like the irresponsible asshole that you are. And that's what I did and I left their house and Carlota didn't say a word, and I knew they were right but I chose to bite my tongue because I wasn't about to admit that I understood. What for?

THEN I SAID TO TOM: Look, Tomás, Tomasito, I had a falling out with Carlota and Manuela because they say you disrespected the cousins' movement and you didn't have respect for anything, and they say that instead of backing them up, I defended you. That's right, I didn't come outside to defend you that night because I was defending you *inside*, I told them you had the right to witness everything because the assemblies had to be women *and* men and not limited to one gender and that if the college girls had a right to influence the movement's direction and to get a say in crucial decisions for us immigrants, even though they're Spanish, then you also have the right! And you did, Tom, Tomasito! And I defended you, I really did. And it's true I didn't tell you, no, I didn't, because I didn't want to act all heroic or make myself into a martyr. You see? And they kicked me out of the house and now I have nowhere to go. And Tom opened his eyes wide and said, in English: Can you repeat that? And I asked: Repeat what? And him: Why didn't you tell me sooner? And me, inching closer to him: I didn't say anything because I didn't want to play the hero. And he said yes, I could stay as long as I needed, but not to say anything to his roommates, because they would want to raise his rent. And I was all, Sure, I won't say a word. And he said, Ok, but talk to the girls because the movement, the cousins, human rights, independence from the Spanish state, fair trade, the republic, democracy, self-determination, armed social movements, the Scottish people striving to be free, and the Irish too, all of them and more, they were more important than me or any individual desire. And we ate salad and tuna and a tomato that was pretty mushy and about to go bad and we went to sleep without sex, because he spent the whole time reading WhatsApp messages about the next protests against the Spanish monarchy and the State and he felt—he really did feel—like he was going to start the revolution and change the world from right there in his bed.

WHAT DO YOU miss most about Mexico? Tom-Tomás asked. I miss my brother. But your brother lives in Madrid. But I miss my brother, the one from Mexico, the one who was little and funny. But you have him, he's in Madrid! Yeah, I know, but I miss the brother from Mexico, not the one in Madrid, because in Madrid he's turned into a good-for-nothing teenager, and he's stubborn and sarcastic and dumb and vulgar. And Tom-Tomás laughed. You're never satisfied! And he caressed whatever part of my body he wanted, mapping my body as if searching for gold under sand. He focused on one part and then another, and, more than erotic, it was like he was an explorer who was astonished all over again at this new world that he liked to contrast with his own: his white skin against mine, dark. Like that, he touched me and then put out his other hand and looked at it and looked at us and he could never get enough of telling me how I was never satisfied. And I lied to him all the time, not because I was a liar, but because I liked to be someone else with him. That's why I talked about Diego and not about what I really missed, which was a lot, which was everything, my grandmother cooking for me, even if there were times when she'd blow a gasket and get all intense, and my grandfather taking me to the movies. And the damp smell in my grandmother's room, because she would rather poison herself with mold than throw out her paintings and things from the past.

And I missed the noise of the street, the music, how loud the cars were, and the tension. Especially the tension, always feeling vulnerable and knowing that the damned emptiness in our stomachs and the insomnia weren't because we felt very sad, but because we lived inside sadness itself. We were all a bunch of sad motherfuckers, and we didn't really know why, though we didn't lack for reasons. On the contrary, so much death and so many disappeared people in the news and so many guys who bullied you in the streets and all because they'd been bullied too, and badly fed and badly fucked and badly loved. I missed the communal feeling of knowing ourselves to be so damn forsaken, and useless, arrogant, but also passionate. Yep, passionate, because in order to survive we needed a whole lot of passion, the passion that comes from hunger, from exhaustion, from discontent. Passion was what made us get up at six in the morning and endure the hateful two-hour traffic, and the noise of the buses, the smell of the person next to us and that other person's bad temper, our stomachs growling at all of us the same. That was what I missed, not because I was a masochist, but because where I was, in Tom's bed or in my mother's house, what you breathed in was a sort of calm that was more like boredom. Europe seemed boring and old and lonely. So many Europeans all together, traveling, shopping, telling each other what to do and how to do it, and all of them old in body and soul, and alone, so alone. Nothing satisfies me, Tom! And I touched his pija, his dick, his verga, and I looked for the scream in him, the racing pulse, the important moment when I could forget that even with all that, all the calm and tranquility and ability to walk in the street alone, even with fucking a white guy, with getting my temporary migration status, I was nothing more than a washer of asses young and old. The one who left their bathrooms squeaky clean.

THINGS STARTED GOING DOWNHILL when I stopped going to Catalan classes. And maybe I wouldn't have quit if the school hadn't replaced my teacher. The first one, Nieves, was tall, with curly hair, very curly, and wrinkles on her face and hands, and a yellow smile that was irresistible. She made us sing in the first class. Sing? Nobody wanted to. And the faces of the youngest students, all embarrassed. There was the guy hiding his face behind his pencil and giggling. Sing? And the girl who was biting her nails, not because she was nervous in that moment, but because she went through life nervous. Sing? And Nieves said yes, yes: *Anem a cantar.* And there we all were, looking at each other but not really seeing anyone, until Nieves said that she would turn off the light and we should focus on the lyrics on the screen. *Anem a cantar tots plegats! Oh! Benvinguts, passeu, passeu, de les tristors en farem fum. A casa meva és casa vostra*, and then all of us were mispronouncing the words and laughing and trying to sing. And Nieves, smiling and singing. And then, as we were all rolling with laughter, we started to talk a little more and to relax, and that's how it was for two, three, four classes, one month, two months. And everything was great with Nieves, but then she broke her leg and asked for a leave of absence. She was gone before the first course was even over. They gave us a pretty half-assed test and moved us all up to the next level, and then a bunch of the students made a WhatsApp group and started suggesting meetups. How we should go to the Venezuelan restaurant, how we should try the Colombian one, let's get some beers with the Arabs at the Sant Antoni market. I went to one of their outings, but I was uncomfortable. It was the first time I'd been in a group with all foreigners that wasn't the cousins. And it made me sad. They all looked like Mexicans, but they were strangers. How if you get the B1 diploma, which takes about ninety hours, then you already have the document for residency, and you can start the paperwork process. How one of them had already gotten a job as a messenger, how another was a driver, and another was working as a sales clerk. How the women—except for me, I claimed to be in school—cleaned floors and worked with some app with a name that sounded like a princess. And how the ones who took care of old women or of children were also taking care of their mothers. All the mothers cleaned houses or waited tables. As the second generation, said the Venezuelan woman, we should be taking a step forward, making something more of ourselves. What is something more? I asked. Well, an easier life. I rolled my eyes at her. Everyone wants to be something more, and they don't even know how to be less. They all gave me weird looks. And I understood. I was saying all that stuff to myself. Because I wanted to be something more than them, though I didn't know what that meant. Like in Mexico, that strange sense of belonging, but at the same time of being a crab in a bucket climbing onto the backs of the others, trying to get out. Fuck 'em all, all except me.

So then I stopped going out with my classmates, but I still looked at their WhatsApp chats every once in a while, mostly on the mornings when Tom went running and I went to clean the houses Martina assigned me. Are you telling those folks to recommend you to their friends? Because this isn't working, Martina told me. I'm giving you jobs for Jimena's sake, but things can't go on like this forever. Yep, got it, I said, kneading my waist and back.

And so, when someone in the WhatsApp group said they were renting out their food delivery account, I said I needed it. I thought you were too busy with school? they asked with smiley-face emojis. Yeah, but I need to work a little, too. And Leandro said ok, it was fine with him, that I could join. And I joined. The days when I didn't have to go clean houses, I set Leandro's status to available. There were three of us, and we divvied up the days so we'd make more or less the same. One euro per delivery, because Leandro kept the rest, or that's how I remember it. Still, Saturdays and Sundays were theirs: one, because they wanted to make more money; two, because those were the days I hooked up with Tom-Tomás. And that's how things were for me: English classes some days, Catalan classes others, cleaning university students' apartments, or riding my bike to deliver fast food.

When Nieves broke her leg and couldn't teach anymore, she was replaced by Gerard, a very old retiree who wore brown and gray vests, who had white hair and was well on his way to bald, and who talked about soccer. But not *just* about soccer, he also talked about being Catalan and how terrible all Spanish words sounded to him. Does this guy realize what he's saying? a blond girl with blue eyes said to me, pissed off but also laughing. Does he even realize? Joder, tía, que pendejo, she said. Pendejo? I thought, short-circuiting. Pendejo? Where are you from? I asked her. From here, tía, I'm from here. And you? I'm from Mexico. No way! I lived there for a long time. What are you doing here? What are you doing after class? she asked. I have to work. Well, you should come out sometime with me and Mario, he's Mexican too! Give me your number, joder, tía, I could really go for some tacos! My name's Nagore! Give me your number, I'm going to tell

Mario to message you next time we go to this Mexican restaurant that's really close to here, she said. And I was pleased because I thought I finally had someone to speak my language with. But the problem was Gerard: every class we had was pure rage. He spent the whole time ranting about everything. Preaching a Catalan purity—puristeando, as some of the students called it. Until one day, in lesson ten, section B, we had to answer this question in Catalan: What would make your neighborhood better? First the Italian guy: More libraries. Then the Venezuelan girl: More bars (laughter). Then the Hungarian girl: Fewer tourists. And the Spanish guy: Fewer immigrants. And all the immigrants: Whaaat? But that *what* was said in silence, because it was more like we were speechless while Gerard wrote our answers on the board in Catalan: "Més bars." But joder, tío, you're not going to say anything to this guy? cried Nagore. We all looked to see how Gerard would react, but Gerard didn't say a thing, or he did, something like how there were a lot of immigrants playing for Real Madrid, too. Nagore slapped the desk and said: Joder, tío, fuck you both! And she picked up her things and left and never came back to class. And after that I didn't want to go back, either. I did go, maybe two or three more times, but then I quit. It bothered me to see Gerard and the Spaniard and the Europeans and the immigrants—*everyone*—just keep going as though nothing had happened, as if that day they hadn't said we didn't belong. I didn't want to go anymore because I wanted to somehow *be* Nagore, but I knew I wasn't, because I wasn't blond and I wasn't brave. I quit Catalan the way I quit everything else I started.

Tía, you're just going to love Mario. He's a great guy. He's Mexican, too. We met at an art show. He was the one who first took me to Catalan classes. Mario? Yeah, he was the short, skinny one in class. Great guy, un tipazo, I'm telling you. You should help me convince him to go back home. Right? The pendejo wants to stay here in Spain without papers. But there's no reason for him to do that, he doesn't need it! This is a guy who's shown his work in exhibitions in Mexico, Argentina, Spain, London, and the dumbass wants to stay in Barcelona. Now you've gotta tell him: don't stay, go home. But why would I tell him that when I live here myself? I asked. Well, that's exactly why! Wouldn't you go back to Mexico if you were a man? As a woman I know you wouldn't, but as a man? Men always have better chances. I don't know, I said, annoyed. They do, they do! she said. Well, I don't know. And Nagore laughed. Don't be mad, I love Mexico, I grew up there! I'd love to go back, but I can't, I just can't. Why not? No, tía, no. Growing up there, seeing how people disappear, no, I just can't. And how they murder women, I said. And her: Yeah, that too, but they murder them here, too, you know, they do it here too. Mario, come here, we're gonna convince you that living in Barcelona is shit!

And there was something about Nagore that I liked, her nearness, her energy, how she always seemed about to break into a smile. How easily she could tell racists to go fuck themselves.

And she said everything to me in my language, with all that pendejo, güey, mamar, all those words I'd stopped using, along with her Spanish from Spain, all that tía and joder, and it made me feel like we were friends, language friends, like I could relax into the feeling and keep talking like myself, without having to pretend I wanted to be neutral. But neither that day nor any other did we convince Mario to accept the idea of going back to Mexico, and he stayed. Nagore was the one who left. Tía, when I have a new phone I'll write you, as soon as I get a new number I'll write you and Mario. You stay strong, so strong! And she left, I think for the Basque Country, where, if I'm remembering right, her dad was from.

WITHOUT THE COUSINS, without Olga and Ainara, without Carlota and Manuela, I only had Tom-Tomás. But it wasn't enough. He wasn't enough. Not his way of being, not his way of fucking. It wasn't enough. Ok, so I don't know English. Ok, so we'll never get married. Why do I stay with him? I wondered, and I told myself that it was because I had nowhere else to go. And I didn't, even though my mother wanted me to go back to Madrid, even though it was on me to go to the cousins and apologize for how selfish I had been, so careless, such an asshole, tan pendeja, pues. And I had a rough time of it because the house cleaning for Martina was more and more sporadic, and delivering food wore me out. First, because the sun made me dizzy, it was so hot and humid, and second, I was on a bike that was too big for me, and I needed to ride it as fast as possible. And if I had to go to Gracia or higher, sometimes I wanted to cry: What am I doing here? Is this what I was born for? Is this what my grandparents raised me for? But I kept on pedaling and I kept on going, that's what I had learned in Spain, to keep going, to keep going, no other choice but to keep going. I went on and I pedaled and I mucked out the houses and washed the piss and shit out of underwear and scrubbed the beer that had been dried on the floor for days, and I pulled hair from drains, and took out the food rotting on the dishes that people let pile up in the kitchen, and even so I couldn't make it to the end of the month; my mom had stopped sending me money because she was paying for therapy for Diego, who had already run away from home twice, and three or four times, I don't remember exactly, he had tried to hit her. Are you going to finish your master's soon? We're barely getting by here, Tom-Tomás said when he saw me take some rye bread from his cupboard. I'm going to pay my share, don't worry, I'd say. And he'd come at me with his fucking sermons about how I had to be thriftier, stop acting like a rich kid and get a job like everyone else. Everyone else? You have it easier than I do! I told him. I practically support you. And him: You don't support me, you contribute to the household. And he kept track of everything: shampoo, use of the washing machine and detergent, the minutes I spent in the shower, the times that his room didn't get swept. But what would I be going back to in Madrid? My mom had more problems with Diego. That's why I stuck it out. And fucked, I fucked a lot, because I really liked Tom-Tomás physically. Because I wanted to fuck and that's it.

Then there was the day that Tom-Tomás told me he had an early band practice, and I said ok, we'd see each other later that night. And then I asked him where the practice was, and he said La Sagrera, as always. So that day I didn't accept any orders in that neighborhood, I played dumb and handed them off to someone else who shared the account with me. But I did take one in Barceloneta, and I even thought, Oh good, I'll get to see the ocean, and I headed out there to deliver four hamburgers. Third floor, no elevator. Apartment A. When I was on my way up I heard music, guitars, the fucking chorus, and I even danced. I swear I danced. While I was walking and putting on the cap with the logo of the app that Leandro lent me and adjusting my pants pockets, I danced. I remember it so clearly. Then the door opened and like we were in a B movie I saw Tom-Tomás playing while one of his bandmates took the food and said something to me in English that I didn't understand but that made everyone laugh, even Tom-Tomás. I saw him turn with a broad grin to see the person they were bullying only to find that it was me, his master's student, wearing the yellow and blue delivery box on my back, and his smile twisted up, yes, but he didn't do anything. He let his buddy tip me while the others handed out the burgers, their burgers, Tom-Tomás's too, and then shut the door on me.

I got out of there fast, nervous and scared that Tom-Tomás would come out after me, so I walked quickly and clumsily and climbed on the bike and started pedaling and I figured that any second I would hear his voice calling my name. But no one was behind me. Tom-Tomás was never behind me, not that day, not ever. Then I stopped for a bit, because I couldn't pedal in the city's hundred-degree heat with tears in my eyes.

I DIDN'T WANT to hash out all the lies, but Tom-Tomás insisted. All of them. I want to know everything, he said. And I cried, more out of shame than real remorse. Like a five-year-old who falls and skins her knees and cries, but more from embarrassment than pain. What have I done to you to make you lie to me? And he was right. But what did I say? Well, I lied because once you tell one lie, then you have to go on lying to maintain that first one. I said it for real, sincerely, but it made Tom-Tomás so mad he punched the wall. You lied too, you're not even vegan! I accused him. How about all those times you made me feel like shit just for wanting to eat a few tacos? You're a hypocrite! And he punched and punched the wall again and shouted god knows what, so many things in very advanced C2 English. I don't want to talk to you, I can't communicate with you, he said in Spanish, and then he switched back to English and yelled at me, stuck his face very close to mine and yelled so loud that he sprayed me with saliva. You still smell like the onion from your hamburger! I told him, as if the nonsense flowed out of me of its own volition and I was powerless to stop it. And to think I wanted to take you to meet my family. Bullshit! he yelled. Who even wants to meet your family, I said. Like I even want to know English, like I even want to be like you. As if I didn't see how you look at me different, how you think I'm the poor little wetback who's managed to get ahead. Pendejo. Asshole. Dickhead. And he kept yelling at me in

English to get out, and he took all my belongings, which weren't many, and threw them on the bed and went to the kitchen and took out three bags from Corte Inglés and started stuffing my things into them. And me, rude to the end: Pinche motherfucking tree-hugger, you throw me out of your house with plastic bags! And I know you pay three hundred fifty euros for this room and you charge me two hundred! Don't think I don't know that! And his white skin turned red and then his ears were red and his arms veiny. Shut up, shut up! I didn't care what you did. I cared about you! Seriously. And I helped him stuff my clothes into bags and I laughed. Oh, how I laughed. And you're still out there singing Vampire Weekend, you fucking wannabe. Vampire! Like the shitty hipster you are. All that "down with the empire," how you're ashamed of your ancestry, and there you are, just bullshitting us, like when you told my brother that you knew a guy who brought Vampire Weekend to his house, which of course is true, you saw them, they were at your friend's house, they played, they were invited. But why tell my brother that? So he'll like you? To show off? Why? We all lie, Tomás, all of us! But Tom-Tomás didn't want me singing to him anymore, ¡Tomás, uuuh, uuuh, Tomás, qué feo estás! He was pushing me toward the door as if I had done something worse than deny my poverty. Would you have even looked at me, Tomás? Would you have fucked me knowing that I'm a delivery girl and that I wash the asses of old people and little kids? Would you? Would you have introduced me to your friends? Would you? And Tomás hesitated. So did I. But then I picked up the bags, opened the door, and left.

THEN CAME THE NIGHTS when I slept on the beach. More because I was a proud pendeja, an arrogant mosquito, than out of necessity. I crept up beside the tourists who were getting drunk and lay down near them. The beach was the only place I could sleep, and only at certain times. There was nowhere else I could go: there were no benches, not a single public place where a human was allowed to lie down and sleep. As if the city had been planned so no one could put their feet up—Screw the homeless! Then I went to clean the houses Martina assigned me and if no one was there I'd sneak a shower, and if I wasn't alone I'd take a spit bath, or I'd do it the French way and use the bidet. But I couldn't go on like that for very long, and I told Martina that if I had to be a live-in, then live-in I would be. You'll like this lady, she's practically mute, doesn't talk anymore, doesn't do anything, she's just waiting around to die. Do you want the job? I said yes. Yes, I'll take an in-house job. And I went to the apartment on Aragó, one of those windowless buildings that gave me claustrophobia. Very pretty location, but old as fuck. Really old, flowered, ugly prints, overstuffed. You know—Spanish. The way only the Spanish can do it. Like the Royal Palace, like the time I went to the Royal Palace with Mom and Diego and Jimena: Ooh-la-la, now ain't this classy! Diego said into my ear as we walked behind Mom and Jimena. Is this what classy is? And the two of us whispering about how awful the monarchy's historical decoration was. *Excusez-moi, madame,* would you allow me to adorn you with this flowery, shit-green print? Diego asked, addressing me with a bow, and I laughed. I shall allow it, my lord. And Mom and Jimena were all, Shhh, shhh, you're embarrassing us. So where's Moctezuma? I don't know, but we'll find him. Screw Moctezuma, I'm hungry. But we did find the statue of Moctezuma, there in the Plaza de la Armería. Well, here we are, asshole, said Diego, and I laughed, because it was true, there we were, even with all the, Oh my, how the Spanish conquest really fucked us over, Oh yeah, the Spanish conquest was the worst. And yet there we were, taking the tour.

So that's what the apartment on Aragó was like. A whole lot of history, hatred, and rebellion, but there we were: the family sponging off the grandmother and the Mexican woman waiting on them, just like five hundred years ago. Who cares whether they're Catalans, Spaniards, Andalusians, whatever, they were all the same to me, just like we were all the same to them. No more and no less.

It's best if you bathe her in the morning. She gets very cold. And this is your room, it doesn't have a window, but since you'll be caring for my grandmother, you'll spend all your time in the living room and there are windows there. I nodded. Take her out for a walk before noon, she hasn't been out in a long time, let's see how she feels. Yes. I said yes. Use anything you need, make yourself at home. Yes, I said, yes. And the granddaughter left, and the old lady and I were alone. It took us a while to speak, more because of me than her. I'm going to bathe you, ma'am, all right? And with her eyes half-closed she said yes and scratched her head. And I put her in the bathtub with warm water and she told me to call her Laura and that's what I called her. Ok, Laura, raise your arm for me and we'll get this over with fast. And Laura's skin was all oily and covered in rashes. How long has it been since you had a bath, Laura? I don't remember. From now on we're going to bathe you every day, ok? And she nodded silently. Oh, it hurts when you put shampoo on me. What do you mean, it hurts? It hurts. And I looked at her closely and said: Let's see. And oh, I saw. Her whole scalp was covered in scabs and some scratches that were still fresh. What happened, Laura? And she shook her head. I felt awful. How was such neglect possible? And I went on rinsing her skeletal body while I thought about my own grandmother. And tears sprang to my eyes, but I pressed my lips together tight and swallowed so I wouldn't cry in front of Laura. Then I wrapped a towel around her and dressed her and we went to the living room so I could brush her hair. Who is taking care of my grandmother? I wondered. Is she ok? Oh, Laura, you have lice. Did you know? And she said yes, she knew. Laura, I'm disgusted by lice, and scared of them. I'm sorry, I'm scared to brush your hair. Don't brush it, don't brush it, just leave it. I'm going to bed. And I lay her down and tucked her in and said: Good night, Laura. And Laura blew me an affectionate kiss and I turned out the light and closed her door. Then I went to the bathroom to check my hair for lice, and all night long I felt my head itching and I wondered what I was doing there.

I'm afraid that Miss Laura has lice. But it can't be! Yes, she does, and I'd like to get rid of them, but there's so little light here that it's impossible. There are places that will do it for ninety euros, I could take her there. That's a lot of money! the granddaughter told me. But your grandmother has lice, and cuts on her scalp, you can't just leave her like that! But it's your job to take care of her. Yes, and that's why I'm telling you I can take her to get it treated. Well, only if you use your own money, she said. I could report you, you know, I blurted out. By then I knew what it meant to stay quiet and accept the humiliation, so I let myself keep going: I can say that you're neglecting your grandmother and that you're paying me under the table. You know that? Or if you want you can fire me, and then I'll get rid of the lice and charge you for it separately. And she was silent as though she couldn't believe I would speak to her like an equal and then she just shrieked: Me cago en tus muertos! and hung up on me. Then, an hour later, she sent me a message to say ok, she would bring me the money in the afternoon, and I could take Laura wherever I wanted. Oh, this is a disgrace, coño! said the de-louser girl when she looked Laura over. Just look at this hive! Poor woman! We're going to get this all taken care of, honey. And Laura looked at us, but her voice was so weak and insignificant that it was drowned out by the sound of the air gun.

I STARTED TO grow fond of Laura. We laughed together. She told me about her life. And she turned ornery when her grand-daughter came to visit, saying to me: Here comes superwoman, the one who can do it all! And I smiled. Yaya, how are you? Are you being treated well? the granddaughter asked. Yes, I'm treated well, what do you want? Well, I've come to see you. Ok, you've seen me, now you can go. And the granddaughter shot me dirty looks because I was a witness to that contempt. Yaya, we want Catalonia to be different for you, too, after everything you've had to go through. And Laura: Nothing for me, thanks, I don't want anything, don't fight for my sake. Let me rest. I've ordered your groceries, they'll be here in a little while, the granddaughter said. Give the account to her, let her order my groceries, we don't need anything from you, go and do your own things. Oh, Yaya, don't be like that. And she turned to me: Can't you go clean the kitchen or something? Don't you see I'm talking to my grandmother? She stays right here, Laura said. And I stayed right there with Laura, but I didn't feel any satisfaction or gratitude, because I really didn't want to be there, much as Laura seemed very nice and very kind and all that. I still didn't want to live that way.

What did you want to be when you were younger? A dancer, Laura said. I had the body for it. See? I was always very thin, and I really liked to dance. But those were different times, it wasn't easy. What about you? she asked. I don't know. My mouth twisted up in shame. The truth is I don't know. But you can do anything. And I shook my head. Is it your mom? My mom is fine. She's not the problem. What is? Why did you end up here? I don't know. I don't know, she imitated me. Learn an occupation, something useful. Just look at my granddaughter, unemployed. A doctorate in political science, and she's getting unemployment. Learn something, get good at something. Aren't I good at cleaning your house? I asked wryly, trying to wriggle out of it. But do something else, don't you want to do something else? she replied seriously, not playing along with my joke. And with my twisted-up mouth, I said yes, I wanted to do something else. And Laura taught me to sew on her electric sewing machine that we got down from the storage space in the bathroom. At least three times a week, she showed me how not to get my finger caught, how to change speeds, and how to design patterns. Laura became my friend, or something like it.

L AURA AND I would go for walks down Calle Roger de Flor and then turn onto Consell de Cent, so I could pass by and see if Martina had hired someone else to clean the apartments I used to cover on weekends, and then I'd send her a message: Don't take away my Sunday slot, don't be like that. And then we'd reach Tetuán and walk all the way down Passeig de Sant Joan to Ciudadela Park. Laura rode in the wheelchair given to her by a neighbor whose daughter had died of cancer a few months before. I'd fitted it with an umbrella to protect her face from sun and wind, and, weather permitting, we would sit and watch the skaters or the musicians who played under the Arc de Triomf. I don't like those people, take me over there, she'd say, when the people who were practicing looked Pakistani or Arab. But they won't do anything to you, Laura, can't you see they're skating and they don't even look our way? They should be at work! she said, and I scoffed. Work? What kind of jobs are they supposed to get? Well, I don't know, I don't know. Not even your granddaughter has a job, Laura, don't be so judgmental. Judgmental, why? I'm not judging them, I'm just telling you to move me over there, look, there. And she pointed someplace far away. Is this why you wanted to be a dancer, Laura? So you could travel the world saying: I don't like those people, take me somewhere else, take me back to Barcelona, to my own people? And Laura eyed me warily and said, Take me home now, I'm tired. Let's go teach you to sew a skirt so you can go travel the world and say you don't like Spaniards.

Laura wasn't like my grandmother, or my mom. She had a sort of peace that I'd never encountered before. But it wasn't a good peace—more like a weary one. As if her body was holding her prisoner, in restraints, and wouldn't let her be. What do you want to do with your life, Laura, besides tell me where to take you on afternoon walks? Me? Nothing anymore, god has forgotten about me. Don't say that. God must think I've died already, he's already put me in a box, he thinks I don't exist. But what do you need? You don't lack for anything, Laura. To die, girl, I've got a real lack of death. Don't say that, Laura. Oh, here I am acting all pitiful for a girl who doesn't even know what to do with her own life. You don't either, Laura, you don't know either. How can you want to die? If you really wanted to die you'd be dead already, I said. Oh, sure, there was a time when I was young, before you were even born, when my husband and I had a very bad argument, right here in this living room—my kids weren't home, they were already gone—and he told me that I weighed him down, that I had always been a thorn in his side, that I was draining his money away, and I said no, don't say that to me, and from then on, because he'd seen how much it hurt me, he said it more and more, and I felt an awful desperation because I thought it was true, but I couldn't leave this house because I didn't have a house of my own; I couldn't leave this life because it was the only one I had, and I often thought about jumping off the balcony, if that's what you mean—of course I've thought about it, many times. What would have been lost if I died? Nothing, I'd just stop spending my husband's money. But I didn't want my children to think I didn't love them. That's why I didn't jump, because I wasn't going to let him win. Understand? If I died, he would win. And I wasn't about to let him win. Sometimes I imagined that if I jumped, I'd mark my body first: It's all Jordi's fault, Jordi murdered my spirit. I'd think about writing that on my chest, but instead I commended myself to god, I put my life in god's hands and here I am, unable to die. It's a good thing you didn't die, Laura. Don't say that, don't say that, because every day I go to bed thinking it will be my last night and every morning I wake up older, tireder, and with the same life as always. Where do you want me to take you on our walk, Laura? To Ciudadela. And just like that, every day, Roger de Flor, Consell de Cent, Tetuán, Passeig de Sant Joan, Ciudadela Park, and every day Laura asked me to move her away from the Pakistanis. Take me over there, she'd say, there, and I would push her as far away as possible, though I always took her home at the same time for dinner.

I FEEL LIKE I can tell you anything; no secrets, you and me. What secrets could I keep from the girl who smells my farts? What shame can I have in front of you, when you're the one who changes my diaper? So, I'm going to ask a question, and you tell me the truth: Which do you think will happen first: I die, or you find a better job? Why are you asking me that, Laura, are you already sick of seeing me in your house every day? And she asked again: When do you think I'm going to die? Not for a long time, I still need you to teach me to knit sweaters, don't leave me in the lurch, I said. Let's set a date, a deadline, let's make a plan, she said. And if I haven't died by that date, you'll help me. Oh, no, don't say that, Laura, don't ask that of me. We can't. Give me a date, any date, just humor me, when do you think? Not for many years. Oh please, come on, give me a date! How about two years, I said. And you'll still be here then? Oh, I hope not, Laura, I would like to be somewhere else. Six months, then, how's that? In six months you'll have another job because I won't exist. Because both of us will be free of this shitty life. Sound good? Oh, Laura, no, don't say that, you're making me sad. Six months. I don't like it, Laura, look, I'm telling you no. Come on, child, don't be dramatic. You're not picking sides, you're not choosing between two things, you're just siding with me. Six months? And with my stomach churning I said yes, six months, although I think I'm against it, I'm against this, I insisted. Don't be sad, it doesn't do any good to get sad now, she said. Now we've made a decision, and you're going to take care of yourself and I will too—you've taken quite enough care of me. I'm saying yes, but I'm against it, Laura, I replied, my voice a little sad, a little relieved, because I was not against it, I wanted her to die, too, because her body was no longer working, and she was looking very tired.

L AURA DIDN'T DIE IN SIX MONTHS, like we'd agreed, she died in eight. We never did make a plan, but after that conversation, we never again said a casual good night. Go on, tell me a dream, I'd say, and she would get into bed and turn out the light and say: Come here, lie down beside me, and she'd start to tell me her dreams. None of them were real dreams, of course, it was all made up, because when it came down to it, I took care of her body, but she took care of my solitude. I dreamed that you went far away, that you didn't live here anymore, that you had a job and didn't need anyone and you never wanted to die. How about you? I dreamed that I knew you before, Laura, back when you were strong, when you believed that the world wasn't going to be like this, and that your life had value. Oh, what a lovely dream, she said. What else? Well, we were friends and not employer and employee. We were friends and we went to Corte Inglés to buy your dresses and stockings and the two of us went by the makeup section and they put blush on our cheeks for us, and then we went out for coffee. A crema catalana, a sandwich, a beer. A cup of coffee. Or maybe a crema catalana, a sandwich, and two beers. And Laura replied: Three, better three beers. So, what else did you dream? Let's see, I dreamed that we were young and lived in France and we were getting laid by a couple of Frenchmen. And she laughed. Do you get laid? Well no, Laura, how could I get laid when I'm always with you? Oh, my dear, so young and so dumb!

and she'd fall asleep, because with every dream her voice and her strength faded and all that remained in her was a very low, almost imperceptible murmur, which always made me go to sleep with the fear that this would be the night her wish came true.

You're so lucky that we're going to be able to blame the government for your death, Laura. You'll see. We'll file a claim and then say it was the medication shortage that killed you. And it will, Laura. How long has it been that they can't fill your prescription anywhere? Almost a month, child. We'll see, maybe this is god remembering I exist. And me, too, I said. But what these fucking pharma companies can't seem to remember is that medicine is for saving lives, not profiting off them. Child, you still believe in people. I'll make you a cup of tea, ok? No, I don't want tea. I don't want it. Have something warm, Laura, it'll do you good. Will you drink it? No, I don't want tea. And she coughed. Her cough was quiet, like the little whistle you hear when an ear gets clogged, a sharp whine, persistent and annoying, but never grating. Then, the almost imperceptible sweetness of old age grew into the noise that strangled her. She couldn't sleep, something was choking her, and she had to cough it up and spit it out. Leave me be, let me suffocate! No, Laura, no! Not like this. Later, we can figure out later how to do it, but not like this. And then she would take the inhaler from me and let me caress her hair. Remember when you had lice? I said, trying to tease her, but Laura asked me to stop, because when you want to die there's no room for laughter. Oh, Laura, should I call your granddaughter, your daughter? No, no. I want to die here, alone, without them and in peace. I don't want to hear about the mistakes I made, or about their mistakes, I want to die here, alone and at peace. Understand? And I said yes, I said yes a bunch of times, until I didn't. It was three in the morning and she started to cough and she coughed and coughed and went on coughing, until I got desperate and scared and called an ambulance. I never saw her again. I never saw her again. I didn't say Goodbye, Laura. I didn't tell her any more dreams, we didn't stick any more pins into cloth for garments we would design together. There was nothing more. No one told me anything, I couldn't go visit her, she vanished. Two days later the granddaughter called me, told me to clean the house, pack up all the dishes, toss all the old stuff, replace the blankets and sheets with new, clean ones. People from a realtor are going to come by because we're going to rent the place out. We'll pay you for the full month, but we'll need you to be gone by the weekend. What about Miss Laura? My grandmother is no longer with us. I felt like shit. Laura could have died at home, in peace, and I had to go and send her to a stupid hospital.

I RAN INTO Tom-Tomás a few times in the street when I was out walking. I was sure of myself, sure of how I felt about him then. But he was still nearby, we practically lived in the same neighborhood, and contrary to popular belief, Barcelona isn't that big. So I would see him in the corner stores where I bought pita bread and he bought his midnight cigarettes. We didn't talk, just avoided meeting each other's eyes. Because we couldn't talk about the lies, the posturing, how we'd made fools of one another for so long. Baby, we don't speak of that, as if we were some real British aristocrats, so polite, never hurting anyone at all. But I think I must have looked pretty rough after Laura's death, because one time he did speak to me. Hey you, how is everything? Fine. What are you up to? Same as always, a dirty ass here, a dirty bathtub there. Same as always. You? All good. Well, great. No, seriously, is everything all right? Yeah, yeah. How's your brother? How's Diego? Fine. And there were other English voices behind him. I've gotta go, he said. Yeah, go on. And he left, got into a car full of English-speaking people, and I stood there looking at him, as though confirming that he would always be fine, and he looked back at me from the window, even rolled it down, and he didn't say goodbye or anything, but he kept craning his neck to stare at me as the car was driving off. Fucking Tom-Tomás, he was never a victim, but neither was I. It was just that we felt nostalgia for something, for the shit we used to say to each other, for the fucks, for sleeping in each other's arms and not feeling alone in Barcelona. Because I don't know what causes it or why, but loneliness is more of a bitch in Barcelona. There the two of us were, looking at each other without saying anything, the dictionary definition of a perfect waste of time. As if all that time our mothers had spent caring for us, or our grandmothers—his grandmother had lived near the bus station, and his parents used to go there after work to pick him and his twin brother up—had been nothing but a bad investment in humanity. Why bother taking care of these two, if in the future they're just going to stare at each other outside a convenience store, incapable of saying goodbye or anything else at all? Is that why we took care of them, just so they could turn out to be so careless?

I TALKED TO Jimena and told her I wanted to go back to Madrid. But why? she asked. I just do, I can't take it here anymore. Oh, a month ago I would have said yes, dear, yes. But you don't want to come back now, I promise you. Why not? I asked. It's your mom and brother. It's mother–son things, things that have to be worked out between the two of them. But what's going on? Oh, nothing's going on, it's just not a good time for you to be here, you took care of your brother long enough, it's your mom's turn now, it's her turn to take responsibility for him, to fight with him, challenge him, educate him. What's wrong, Jimena? Nothing's wrong, dear, but you're not going to find what you're looking for here, if what you want is a family—you're not going to find that here right now. And I don't know why, but I believed her. Or more like I trusted her blindly because she might have been right, because I *had* taken care of Diego for a long time, I had supported him enough and I'd coddled him enough. It was true, or true enough, that it was a two-person problem, a thing between mother and son. A mother who wanted to be a mother and a son who didn't want to be a son. Not like before, when I was there, when she didn't want it and he did. Maybe it was better that way, for them to work things out on their own. And so I listened to Jimena and made peace with the idea of giving them freedom and of feeling free myself. And I stuck with Martina and cleaning her apartments on Sundays while I waited to find another live-in job. Until Olga, who seemed to feel sorry for me, told me that no, I'd done my time as a live-in, and she offered to let me take care of the kids she watched during the week, because she had a full-time job at a hotel on the beach in Castelldefels. And I said yes, and she offered to let me live with her, Ainara, and another girl named Isabel. You can live with us, pay for the smallest room, and help us out when we have too much work. What about Martina? Screw Martina, she's had us by the throat for too long now. No more. And the four of us went to live together in Sants, in a building close to the train station, so the cousins' meetings were right on our way. At long last, for better or for worse, I was a cousin.

I WENT BACK to attending the cousins' meetings, but neither Olga nor I really liked the college girls who were always around, doling out advice. What's with them? Do they really think they're going to take down the hotels with their tweets? And I laughed. Yeah, what's *with* them? All those videos, all that "Long live the cousins," "We're all cousins here," but they're not cousins. Don't worry about them, they're fighting their little fight. What fight? You think that after the March 8 protest they ever invited us to anything again? Nope, they stuck us out in front, let us talk, said bravo, and then everyone went their separate ways. You'll see, if no one's pissing in the streets or showing off their pubes, it's not their revolution. Wanna bet? And we bet. Olga said they wouldn't be at the march on Thursday: They won't go, we'll be there with the same three suckers as always, with our slogans and everything, but no sign of any college girls. They won't go. Wanna bet? And we agreed that if the college girls showed up and brought others who were moved by the cause, Olga would pay for my beers that Wednesday when we went dancing at the Cuban bar. And that's what we did: I went to take care of the kids I had that day, then met Olga to get something quick to eat on Las Ramblas, and we went from there to Diagonal Mar to join the cousins in their protest. It made us laugh to see them there, all alone, the same three suckers that Olga had predicted, plus the other cousins, no more than fifteen total, talking amongst themselves, cheering each other on. Making videos and taking photos and waiting the wait, the farce of waiting for someone from the hotel that had fired them to come out and talk. Cracking jokes but with shrill voices, like when you're pretending to be ok but you're not.

Olga and I took a cab there since we were running late, and when we arrived and swung the car door open, I pretended to be horrified to see them out in public in their cleaning-lady uniforms, rubber gloves on their hands, in character for their roles playing themselves. And with my exaggerated shock that was also very real, I started making fun of them. But the funniest part was the fact that I had lost the bet and I didn't have money to go dancing at the Cuban bar with Olga; in fact, I didn't even have money to get home, because that day the woman who let me watch her kids didn't have change and she'd asked if she could just pay me next time. So, at the horror of seeing us there, so few of us, so overlooked, so invisible and penniless, I could only laugh and join in and let them take photos so that on the Twitter account managed by the Spanish students it would seem like there were a lot of us and we were on the warpath. Baby, we don't talk about this, but how I wished I could go off to Tom-Tomás and be or at least feel like the real aristocrat he had always wanted me to be.

W

HO KNOWS HOW the neighbors thought of us—
as panchitas, Latinas, a nuisance, a stain on their
neighborhood that couldn't be washed away—but
they never said a word, nothing, not until Diego came to visit.
This is not a hotel, said a bald, pot-bellied man who smelled like
tobacco. I ignored him and grabbed Diego's arm and we went
outside. What's with that pendejo? Well, he's a pendejo. Just
ignore him. We're going to take the metro and this time we won't
get lost. Diego laughed and said ok. We went to the beach: we
bought sodas at a shop, said hi to the clerk who gave me his left-
over bread at the end of the day, and I bought Diego the ham-
flavored chips that were his favorite now, because you couldn't
get adobadas here. All we need now is some Valentina hot sauce. I
know, but I brought some apple with piquín chile. Hell yeah, you
know what's up, he said. And I did know. I had been there with
Diego through all his likes and dislikes, from when he wrinkled
his nose the first time he tried lemon to when he wolfed down his
first Abuelita chocolate. Do you go to the beach a lot? No, not so
much. The other day I went with the cousins, but it was for a protest, imagine that. Yeah, I can picture it. So what do you think, do
you like it here? And Diego shrugged. It's the same, wherever you
are it's the same thing, you're always just surviving. I don't think
so, Diego, there are some nice things here, Barcelona isn't like
Madrid, or like Mexico. I know, but it's the same everywhere:

we work to live and then we live to work. Everywhere, always. Oh, what do you know about working, pendejo. We stuck our tongues out at each other.

Our grandmother had taken us to the beach many times, usually to Acapulco, because my aunt Carmela's husband had a friend who had a timeshare in one of those hotels that used to be a luxury resort. My mom and grandfather never came, but my grandmother, Diego, and I went every once in a while, whenever our abuela got the whim. Go on, pack your clothes, tomorrow we're going to Acapulco. Tomorrow? But tomorrow's a school day! We're going to Acapulco anyway! And we went. We didn't even tell my grandfather, we just left early with our backpacks emptied of school supplies and stuffed with clothes, and we took a cab to Taxqueña. Most of the time we'd find tickets for buses leaving soon, but sometimes we did have to wait. See, Abuela, you should have bought them in advance, we're just wasting time and I'm already hungry. And I don't know how we weren't knocked out by the five- or almost six-hour bus ride, maybe it was the anticipation, the excitement, the thrill of breaking the rules and getting out of our routine, of leaping into the waves so they'd knock us over and our grandmother would warn us not to get so far out, to stay on the shore. That's how it was that time Diego visited me, too. It took me a few months to save up for his ticket, but I bought him a trip to Barcelona that summer. Just for a weekend, because he hadn't passed all his classes and Mom had grounded him. You shouldn't give that little fucker anything. It's more for me than for him, Mom. You should pay me back all that money I lent you instead of encouraging the little shit. Just one weekend, I'll pick him up at the station, and I'll send him right back to you. Ok? Suit yourself; if it were up to me, I'd have him locked in his goddamn room to see if he'll finally get bored with scratching his own fucking balls. He has to leave at nine in the morning, and it'll take nine hours, I'll let you know when he's here. But we didn't let her know, and I don't know why, whether it was our revenge for when she used to keep us waiting days for her calls in Mexico, or because deep down we didn't really believe she was waiting to hear from us.

How are things? Fine, he said, just fine. Fine, my ass. If only they were fine. Shut up, dummy, is that what you invited me here for? And I ran my hand over his hair. You need a haircut. Damn, you and Mom really know how to nag. Who cares about my hair? It's summer, anyway. Well, that's why you should cut it, you'll be cooler. Nope. Hey, remember that time we threw sand at Abuela and she got mad and made us go back to the hotel? And then the laughter, we laughed a lot that visit. Remember when she was watching that telenovela at the hotel and she said: "I used to hate facial hair, but then it grew on me?" And more laughter. We laughed at our grandmother, at everything we could think of, we delved deep into our memories, as if we both knew we had to really make the most of that time and laugh, because alone— that is, without each other—we were quieter and didn't feel like cracking jokes, didn't feel like being ourselves, the kids who laughed their asses off the moment they saw each other.

Damned sand, it itches, huh? Oh, calm down, pinche Mister Cancún, quit your bitching. Damned sand, it itches, I imitated him. So, are you going to stay here forever? In Barcelona? Yeah. No, I don't think so. Don't get the idea it's all so easy here. And I do feel lonely, because the cousins are all fine and good, but I don't know, I don't fit in with them, I said. I know, he said, I get it. But there's nowhere else to go. Maybe there is, I said, but we just haven't thought of it yet. There isn't, he said gravely. But I insisted: Maybe there is, maybe someday, together, we could find a way, you never know, maybe we could go live together, work hard and go someplace else. Get away from Mom, you mean? Well, yeah, I said with a shrug. But didn't we supposedly want to be *with* Mom? he asked, and we looked at each other mockingly and laughed and then he threw sand in my face and ran off to the water, while I shouted: Oh, you little asshole, you're gonna get it, you'll see! And we saw, we saw each other like when we were little, out in the waves and shrieking at the cold water and splashing each other in the face while people shot us dirty looks and we went on laughing, even though our grandmother wasn't there to tell us to stay close to the shore.

I wanted to take Diego to meet Mario, so he could see himself through Mario's eyes. Look at Mario, I planned to say, just look at this pendejo, he stayed here without papers, even though he's a painter, an artist with exhibitions, with connections, and the pendejo is here, trying to find a way to apply for residency. You, I planned to tell Diego, you have an opportunity, you have papers thanks to Mom, so take advantage of it, study, finish high school and make something of yourself. Look at this dumbass pendejo, I was going to insist, even with all the opportunities he has, here he is, doing a little job here, another one there, fighting me for the delivery gig, all so he doesn't have to go back to Mexico. But I didn't get to say any of that, because Saturday morning Olga wanted me to cover for her and take care of some kids in Gracia. But Diego is here, can it wait? Whatever, she said, while the three of us were eating breakfast standing up in the kitchen. I thought you needed the money, but if you can't do it, I'll ask someone else. You know how it is with these women, you have to get them to trust you, they need to know you're there. And I really wanted to take Diego to have lunch with Mario, but I said yes anyway. Then Olga left, and although Diego and I had just been chattering about the Barcelona match, now we went quiet, staring at the floor, avoiding each other's eyes. So, you can take a shower, watch TV if you want, I'll be back in a bit. Sure, he said. What? Nothing, he said, smiling that fucking asshole smile of his that he got whenever he was being sarcastic. What? What do you mean, what? That's what I'm asking, what are you looking at me like that for? Nothing. What? Seriously, what? Nothing, fuck. Tell me. Nothing. Tell me. Is this what you came here for? he asked. Is this why you left home? Asshole, pendejo, I said. You're the asshole, pendeja. You're the pendejo. Pendeja. What do you know, you little brat pendejo? You're the pendeja. What do you know, pendejo, you can't even pass your fucking classes, so what do you know? Pendeja, you think you can just go through life acting like a pendeja the way you do? Pendejo, what do you know? Pendeja. Shut up, pendejo. Pendeja, you're the pendeja. Oh, yeah, there's nowhere to go, oh yeah, the world is shit; tell me something I don't know, pendejo, I said. You're the pendeja, he said. Then what are you, pendejo? And you? Pendeja. You're the pendejo. How the hell are you going to make a living, with that fucking pendejo face of yours? Or you think everything is just going to be handed to you forever? Pendeja, he said. I may be a pendeja, but I'm the one who brought you here. See? You're just like Mom, both of you pendejas, throwing yourselves on the floor to get it dirty just so you can clean it up. And I opened the door, furious, but I turned around looking at the clock and told him to keep an eye on his phone, that he should be ready to go whenever I messaged him and we'd see if we could still catch up with Mario for lunch at the Mexican restaurant. He didn't say anything, just flopped on the sofa and turned on the TV. I closed the door and went to the elevator and burst into tears, because it did hurt, because I did feel bad, because he was right and I didn't have any real reason to be living the life I was living, and I really did feel like a pendeja.

W E DIDN'T GO to the beach that Saturday. We ate dinner at home, because the three hours I supposedly had to spend watching the kids in Gracia turned into seven. Diego texted to tell me he was going for a walk, and I told him to take some money from my drawer, explaining exactly where the roll of bills was, and I asked him to put the rest back. Just take twenty, and go look for a Barça souvenir, you might find something. He replied with a gif, and I went on watching a movie with the kids I was taking care of. But then in a flash I remembered what had happened in Madrid. I jumped up from the couch like I was on a springboard, saying I was going to the bathroom, and I called him. He answered right away. Where are you? By the Sagrada Familia, there are souvenir stores around here. What did you eat? Nothing, just the sandwiches you told me to eat. That's all? Yeah, the sandwiches, that's what I said. How much money did you take? I asked. Hey, I gotta go, it's hard to hear and my phone's about to die, he said, and hung up. I felt the tingling in my stomach, always my stomach. And I was restless after that. I got home and he was still out, so I went to the drawer to check the money. There was a lot less than I'd had in the morning. Diego hadn't taken twenty euros, he'd taken more. Son of a motherfucking bitch, I thought. And his thick voice in my head: Pendeja. Well, that *is* what he thinks of me, he tells me so all the time! I thought, and I was well and truly pissed. Then

Olga and Isabel came home with food from a banquet they'd worked at the hotel, and they invited me to sit down and eat with them. Diego came in later, and by then I was a little drunk and didn't want to say anything. But we both knew we knew. We avoided each other all night, both acting as if the other one didn't exist, our eyes never meeting. But he was laughing it up with Isabel, and Olga was saying god knows what to me, but I didn't hear her, I was only thinking about Diego, about how I had him right there but he wasn't Diego anymore. He was no longer the Diego I had taken care of, the Diego who respected me. He wasn't that kid anymore, he was this other Diego; no longer the curly-haired gap-toothed boy who would lunge at me and hug me and ask me to race him to the corner by our house, the kid I'd always let win. He wasn't that Diego anymore, he was another one now, one I didn't know and couldn't get to know. Diego, running away right in front of us, in front of Mom and me, he was leaving right in our faces, and we let him run far away, believing that in spite of everything, he had nowhere else to go, and he'd come back. We always thought he would come back.

I WENT WITH Diego to the Sants train station. We didn't talk, but my stomach made noise. My stomach, always my stomach. Diego was wearing the Barcelona cap he'd bought, and it hid his eyes. You have everything, your ID? Yeah, he said. You have the sausages for Mom? Yeah. You know how long the trip is? Nine hours. You have the ticket? Yeah. Let's see it, I said, and he showed me his phone. The screensaver was a picture of him with two guys and a girl, Marina, making funny faces. Are those your friends? Yeah. And above, the bar along the top, the music player on pause. Vampire Weekend on pause. Then we checked the train's route, several stops, a transfer. Your phone is charged? And he took a charger cable from his pocket. Ok. And silence.

What Mom's into doesn't bother me, in case you were wondering, I told him. And he smiled, but said nothing. What time is the train again? Oh, it's leaving soon, he said, looking at the electric sign on the wall. You want any snacks for the trip? And he pulled a bag of ham-flavored chips from his pocket. We smiled, genuine smiles. I took that moment to hand him the bottle of piquín chile I'd brought with me: Here, I can't use it anymore. He shook his head. Take it, it's bad for my stomach, you saw how I spent all last night in the bathroom. You'll be doing me a favor, it's not a gift or anything. And Diego took it and put it in his backpack. We avoided each other's eyes. Are you going to send Abuela the photos from the beach? He said yes. Make sure you send her that one of us at the port, so she can see what it's like. He said ok. Are you going to let me know when you get there? Yeah, but I'm gonna be really tired, maybe tomorrow or something. No, Diego, tell me when you get home, please. And he said ok. Then he looked back at his phone and started tapping on it and ignored me for a while. The two of us, standing there in silence among the crowd, ignoring each other. It was half an hour until his train left. You want something, a bottle of water or a sandwich? I asked again. Nope, I don't want anything, thanks, he said as he laughed at something on his phone. Should we sit down? No; he said no. Actually, I'll just go, better to get inside before there's a long line. You sure? Yeah. And I went closer as though to give him a hug, but we both moved awkwardly and didn't give each other a chance. Where's the line? he asked, as though disoriented. Over there, I said. And he pulled up his train ticket, tugged the cap down farther over his eyes, and held on to the straps of his backpack as though to show me that his hands were very busy and he couldn't hug me. Well, see you soon, huh? Maybe I'll be there for Christmas, I said. Yeah, sure. Forget everything you've done and start over, I told him. But his eyes were saying no, as if he'd given up, as if he had stopped fighting, as if he had laid down his weapons. He just made a gesture that I didn't understand and said, Bye. I stood there waiting while they checked his ticket and put his backpack through the metal detector. Then I saw him as he was: Tall, broad-shouldered, nearly a man. I waited for him to turn around and look at me so I could wave goodbye, my hand hanging in the air, ready to respond as soon as he looked back. But he didn't look back, and the last I saw of Diego was his broad back, his five-foot-seven figure moving off until I could no longer make him out in the crowd. I never imagined that would be the last time I'd see him alive. I would have liked to tell him: You have such a bright future, keep going, keep going, keep going . . . But Diego didn't keep going.

THAT MORNING Diego left Barcelona to go back to Madrid, I got up early because I couldn't sleep. I'd stayed in the living room so Diego could sleep in my bed and not bother Olga or Isabel if they got up early. My head hurt because we'd bought a two-euro bottle of red wine the night before, and I was in a hurry to be drunk so I wouldn't start accusing Diego of stealing my money and turning into a real pendejo. I was mad, truly betrayed and hurt, with a real goddamn urge to slap him upside the head. But I didn't; I decided to toast some bread instead, squeeze some orange juice, and wake him up so that we could take a walk along the beach before he left. He agreed and got up and went to the bathroom and put on his boots and said he was ready. Shameless little slacker, I thought, and my stomach burned and my head throbbed, but I was the one insisting on going to the port, where the statue of Columbus was.

Look, there's the pinche explorer who discovered you, I said, pointing at Columbus immortalized, gazing out to sea. Diego made a face at me. This is where kids your age come to skate. They also go to the Arco de Triunfo. You remember seeing that yesterday? He said yes. Then we stopped at a shop and he told me he needed to buy some smokes. Cigarettes? Yeah, he said, and it was like he'd suddenly realized he was naked, flaunting himself, something between proud and ridiculous. I didn't say anything, but I got even madder. You really are a shithead, cabrón, I thought. Then we got to the beach, looked for a spot far away from other people, and sat down to take off our shoes and look out at the water. Why did you steal that money from me? I was already giving you twenty fucking euros, why did you take more? I didn't take anything, leave me the fuck alone. What do you mean you didn't take it? Don't fucking lie to me, I had more money in the drawer, don't be a such a dick, the least you can do is admit it. Why did you take it? Diego wouldn't look at me. I'm telling you I didn't steal anything, fuck! What for? Tell me what you took it for. But I couldn't get anything out of him. Diego was like the damn Columbus statue, stone-faced, passive, looking out into the beyond with such a fucking air of superiority that it drove me crazy. Don't even think I don't know you were the one who took Mom's money that time, pinche culero, and you let her think it was me. I didn't take anything. Stop lying, you fucking asshole! Just admit it, be a fucking man, have the fucking balls to say it was you! And he took out a cigarette and lit it right there, not looking at me. You're not going to admit it? I'm talking to you, at least talk to me, god-fucking-dammit, don't make me sit here talking to myself like a dumbass. You think I didn't know it was you? Who else could it be? You think I believed that fucking story that I was the only one who went into Mom's room that day? I *saw* you go in a bunch of times, Diego: I went to the bathroom and clear as day I saw you sneak in and search Mom's drawer; don't even pretend you didn't, because you snuck into my room too. One time, I saw you pick up the box I had on my dresser and take some coins and then you practically tiptoed out. And don't tell me you don't remember, because you do: I asked you what you were doing in there and you played the dumbass, but we both knew you had gone into my room and taken my money. How could I not know it was you who took Mom's cash? It wasn't me, goddammit. It *was* you, Diego, have some fucking balls, god-dammit, why do you steal, asshole, you think money falls from the fucking sky? Now you're really talking like Mom. Why did you take my money? Give it back. I need it. What money? Fuck, what money? You told me to take twenty euros and that's what I took, he said. I felt desperate and smacked my hands on the sand. Admit it, goddammit! Just admit it! You're getting fucking delusional now, just like Mom. Fucker, you fucking ungrateful little asshole. Oh, so you're gonna cry now? he said. Asshole, I said. Why didn't you tell on me if you were so sure I took Mom's money? Maybe it *was* you! I mean, what money did you leave with the day she kicked you out? Did you really have so much cash saved up? Don't be so fucking cynical, Diego. Why didn't you tell Mom it was me if you were so sure? he asked again. You're admitting it, asshole! Right? All you do is spout bullshit, just like Mom. You don't know who to blame for something—Diego did it. Always fucking Diego's fault. You don't know how to deal with your frustration—Diego, must be fucking Diego's fault. You don't know what to do with your lives—Diego, the one who ruins our fucking lives is Diego. Don't say that, we've always taken care of you, we've always worried about you. Yeah? Where were you when Mom beat the shit out of me to defend her fucking girlfriend. Where? What girlfriend? Jimena, the nosy bitch who never stops busting my balls. Everything Jimena says, Mom listens to. If I drink milk, it's why did I drink it all; if I make something to eat, it's why did I make a mess; if I wash my clothes, it's why did I waste detergent. I'm fucking sick of it! You, Jimena, Mom! Fucking hysterical old bitches. I wanted to hit him, and I tried, but he wouldn't let me. His hand was twice the size of mine, same as his body. He caught my wrist and pushed it away from him in one motion, and I almost fell on my face in the sand. Motherfucker! I said. Goddammit, now I guess *you're* going to say I hit you. Fuck this, I can't take it anymore, you can all go fuck yourselves. And he got up and started to leave, brushing the sand from his boots, and I sat there looking at him and not knowing what to do, because I wanted him to leave, because he was a motherfucking liar, a goddamned thief, a freeloader, a thoughtless fucking teenager who didn't take responsibility for his actions; but at the same time he was Diego, my brother, the little boy who stuck his hand in his mouth when he didn't want to say anything and sucked on it as if he wanted to gulp it down and eat himself and disappear. Swallow himself whole. He always wanted to swallow himself whole. And I told him to stay. I said: Come on, sit down, don't go. And he snorted, and I said: Come on, you're about to leave for Madrid, just sit down. And he sat down and I got even madder, because I would have liked for him to have a little fucking dignity, for him to be able to say, truthfully, No, it wasn't me, I didn't steal your money. And not only did I not steal from you, I didn't steal from Mom either, I don't steal, I don't lie, you're both wrong about me, I'm Diego. But Diego sat down and took a bottle of horchata de chufa from his backpack and started to drink it, and he asked me if I wanted some and I shook my head and he replied that this shit tastes like ass, that he'd bought it the day before because he'd thought it would taste like the rice horchata in Mexico, but instead it tasted like shit; but he kept on drinking it, and then he took out another cigarette. How did you buy horchata, cigarettes, and a cap with only twenty euros? And he froze. But not from fear, he froze in exasperation, and he just sat there staring at me and then picked up his boots again and walked off to the sidewalk and when I saw him putting on his boots to leave, I started going after him and he didn't even wait for me, I had to run to catch up.

And that was how I remembered Diego: shameless Diego, cold Diego, Diego the liar, the asshole who had stolen my money and who stole money from our mother. That's the way I remembered Diego while I was on the train to Madrid after he killed himself: cynical, passive, adolescent, a real son of a bitch, and I cried and cried, even though everyone looked at me weird, and I made their train trip pretty uncomfortable.

PART THREE

WHEN DIEGO WAS LITTLE, my grandmother and I knitted him a rainbow blanket. Diego wanted to bring it with him on the plane to Madrid, but we had to explain that he couldn't. He insisted he would get cold. I told him that they handed out blankets to passengers on planes. I shot down all his arguments. We compromised by saying we could get the blanket next time we went to Mexico to visit our grandparents. When I got to their house carrying Diego's ashes in a plastic bag, there was the blanket in the bedroom, just like we'd left it. There were pins fastened to it, holding on some pictures that we'd planned to iron on. I swallowed hard. It was all real. Diego was dead.

Y MOM WAS with Jimena resolving things, paperwork, misunderstandings, making decisions about some bullshit here and some bullshit over there. Mexico or Spain, coffin or urn for his ashes? How, what papers do we need, what papers do we not need? And meanwhile, I was in Diego's room hunting for his smell. Everything still, untouched, dirty, spills on the table, the headboard dusty, socks thrown in the laundry basket. And his closet a mess, lived in, as if my brother were about to come in at any minute to change his shirt.

I understood Diego. Ever since we got to Spain we'd been like amputees with no diagnosis. Like we were missing something, but everyone denied it. Missing something? Au contraire! We had gotten everything: House, papers, mother! What could possibly have been amputated? Well, Mexico, I thought. They've cut off our Mexico. But not Mexico the country, Mexico as a yearning. As what in Portuguese they call saudade. You get sick, you come down with saudade, you die a little. How could I not understand Diego?

What pisses you off the most about living here? I asked him once. That I don't get to dance, he told me. We never dance anymore. And it was true, we had stopped dancing. Our grandparents' house was far away, we had no place to crank the music all the way up, no hot food: there was no more childhood, we had ceased to be. And although we tried to repeat the scenes, the music, the moments, we were no longer what we'd been before. No one taught us how to grow up. Diego was like an old double bass—inconvenient, noisy, bulky—that I didn't know how to take care of. I was a clumsy music student who couldn't hold him up. That's how I felt, like I'd flunked out of music and out of life.

Sometimes I feel like instead of a mom, we have a daughter, like we're the ones who have to take care of her, Diego said to me every time Mom came home from work pissed off, angry and yelling at us over every little thing. Well, so what, Diego, so what? I'd reply. She's suffered, too, she's lonely, too. So what, he retorted. If she's not going to be my mom, she could at least not be a burden. I sighed and shook my head at him, but he was right. At those moments, at least, I thought he was right.

Jimena was the one who asked me to take Diego's ashes to Mexico. She brought it up while we were sitting on my brother's bed. He's going to be cremated? I asked, snapping back to reality. Yes, Jimena said. Why doesn't Mom go? Your mom is in no shape to travel, I can't even get her out of bed, she won't even go to the bathroom, she's shattered, dear. I'm shattered too, I replied, refusing to let my grief be amputated, not this time. Your mom is our burden to carry now, and it will make everything harder . . . Help me, Jimena pleaded. And I grabbed Diego's phone and clutched it to my chest, holding on to god knows what. My mom has always been a burden, I said. And Jimena didn't say anything, didn't try to deny it.

THE DAY BEFORE I left for Mexico, I spent the night in Diego's room. Listening to his music. Searching through his phone. Until morning. There wasn't much: a few photos, a few messages. He'd left it clean. The photo with Marina and his other friends wasn't his screensaver anymore. He had erased it all: email, apps, everything; maybe he thought no one else would do it for him. He didn't wait for us.

Diego didn't leave us clues, no goodbye letter, no message. He saved us the trouble of trying to find out the truth, because no one was going to give it to us. One of the few times he talked to me while I was in Barcelona, he asked me to list off the people we should be grateful to. I didn't think much about it: the grandparents? I replied. No, I mean here in Spain. Jimena? Your friends? What are you asking, Diego?, what is it you want to thank people for? And he was quiet for a moment, until he said: Exactly, there's nothing to be grateful for. Mom? I kept trying. Yeah, Mom, he said, but he was no longer interested. I hadn't said what he'd wanted to hear.

How's school going? I asked, to see if he would give me any more clues. All good, the same asshats supposedly "teaching" classes, the same fuckers who fall asleep in what's supposedly a "school"; it's all the same, sometimes I feel like never going back. But you have to, I told him. Yeah, yeah, I'll go to school every day of my life, I'll become the clown everyone wants me to be. You're impossible, Diego García. Yep, he told me, I am. I'm impossible. Diego, listen, don't expect people to give you things, don't wait around for that. Silence. Can you hear me, Diego? What did you say you wanted? he demanded, why'd you call me? And then he hung up, but I didn't realize and I kept repeating: Can you hear me, can you hear me? until I got off the metro and called him back. He didn't answer, I got his voice mail. Diego never waited, he always did what he wanted, like erasing anything from his phone that could give us a clue, other than the music playlists. Four albums, forty songs, all by Vampire Weekend.

A RE YOU EXCITED about going to Madrid? my grandmother asked Diego. No, I'm not excited, should I be? That day, Diego was packing up the clothes he wasn't going to take and putting them in boxes. My grandmother said she was going to donate them. She didn't donate anything. When I saw the rainbow blanket she'd knitted, I knew she hadn't given any of it away. Boxes and bags of Diego's clothes and mine were in the closet of the room where we'd slept with Mom. Photos hung on the walls, Diego's toys, his kindergarten drawings—it was a kind of altar. My grandmother inadvertently turned that room into an altar. A premonition: Diego always had to be venerated, ever since he'd been born and had granted our mother the status of a respectable woman. Diego, our grandparents' favorite, the orphan who'd had a dad. All Diego.

I left his ashes there, in that room, until my grandparents could buy an urn that was worthy of my brother. I felt angry. As if with Diego's death I was being erased. Or else relegated to the same position I'd always had: none. I was Diego's sister, his supporter, the plastic bag that carried him on the plane, Madrid, New York, Mexico. The mode of transportation, the carrier who took him from Abuela to Mom, from Mom to Abuela. A mere messenger.

I'm not excited, Diego, should I be? I loved you, but you loved the sea. Who will cry for me when they're all busy crying over you? That's what I was thinking as I opened the little wooden box and touched your ashes. Just a little, just enough to smudge my fingers. Is this the fate the world planned out for us? Then my grandmother came in asking if I was ready to recite the rosary. Out of fear she would see me with my brother on my hands— caught Diego-handed—I licked my fingers. I ate my brother. I thought that if I were to ever ask to be reborn, no one would agree to it. But with Diego they would, they would all clamor for Diego to be born again. I didn't pray at all, I never was a believer.

D URING THE NINE DAYS of rosaries for Diego, the neighbor ladies asked me about Madrid. How's Madrid? How are you doing in Madrid? Do you have a boyfriend yet? It's fine, thanks. It's fine: I'm just here, thinking about how I'd rather be tied to some train tracks. It's going great, ladies, and how are things with you?

Things were not good with them. They didn't need to tell me; I could see it. Our tattered clothes spoke for us. We'd never looked so poor as we did that day. Why *wouldn't* people call us panchitas, when that's what we were? Ragged, beleaguered strays. How's Joana? I asked Joana's mother, a neighbor of my grandmother's who'd watched us all grow up. Joana? she replied, as if I had asked her about some mythical being. Come here, help me bring out more tamales! my grandmother called to me. I obeyed and went to the kitchen to take out the sweet tamales. My grandmother motioned for me to be quiet. Why, what happened to Joana? Shhh, shut up, she said, pinching me with her voice. What? I can't ask questions? Joana's gone, a lot of things have happened since you left. Where did she go? We don't know, we still don't know, but someday we'll find out. You think people haven't moved an inch since you left? Things move on here. Don't ask questions you don't want to know the answer to.

Joana was kidnapped by some ex-military men in a gray truck. She had gone out for tortillas at three in the afternoon. One of the men who took her was her ex-boyfriend, and so the bystanders figured they were having a lovers' quarrel, and that was why she resisted getting into the truck. They never heard from her again, and some people think she's dead, others that they took her to Tlaxcala, because that's where the ex-boyfriend's family is originally from. No one has said anything to the ex's family; they're still in the neighborhood, acting like nothing happened. Everyone knows that when someone is discharged dishonorably and then has money, it's because their allegiances have changed; now they're no longer military, but they work both sides, the military and organized crime. My uncle told my grandmother not to get involved, because this was serious and she shouldn't put herself in danger, and now no one talks about Joana, not even her own mother. They say that the ex-boyfriend's brother struts around with his gun in his pants, and he doesn't have to say a word for us to know everything. It's a military weapon, so he's clearly well connected. My grandmother says that Joana's brother asked for a transfer to Tlaxcala so he could look for her, but they still haven't found her. You think someone dying on you is the worst thing that can happen? my grandmother asked me. Is that what you think? Diego is here, with us, in the place he never should have left. But what about Joana? How can we pray for her? What can we ask god to do for her?

G ETTING DEAD IS worse than getting drownded, right? Diego asked us the first time he went into the ocean and felt like water was getting into him everywhere. My grand-mother cracked up laughing. I cracked up, my aunts and uncles cracked up. Not my mom, because she was already in Spain by then. Diego liked the ocean more than anything else back then, and that's why my aunt gave him swimming lessons, because you could really tell he enjoyed it. Poor little thing, no dad and no mom. Let him go swimming, it doesn't cost that much. And my grandfather took him on Tuesdays and Thursdays, from five to six in the evening, while I stayed home to finish my home-work before he got back and wanted to do things I would have to watch him doing. Is getting dead worse than getting drown-ded? I'd ask while I bathed him, or teased him, or fed him dinner. And Diego laughed and said yes: I'm not going to stop swimming just because I drown. I'm going to fly in the water. But be careful, make sure you don't die, I'd say. No, I'm not gonna die, he assured me, downing his chocolate bread with milk. Do you think that if we die we go to heaven? No, I don't think so, I told him. Do you think your dad's in heaven? No, my dad is in the ground, that's where they put him. And that's where we're gonna be too. No such thing as heaven. So we fly underground? Yeah, there you go, we're going to fly underground, I said. Do you believe in heaven? No, I don't believe in heaven, Diego, finish your bread. What do you believe in? Nothing, we just die and that's it, I told him. We just die . . . I hope I've flown before that happens. Yes, Diego, if you put your mind to it, I'm sure you'll fly. Does Mom believe in heaven? No, she doesn't believe either, we're not believers. *I* believe, he told me proudly, because I see it every day with these eyes that are mine and not yours. I hope Diego died believing in heaven. I hope.

ALL I TOOK to Mexico of Madrid Diego was his ashes, his defective phone, and a shirt I started to sleep in every night. The first few days I messaged my mom to see how she was doing, but she almost never answered, so I stopped. Who cared about my mom? My mother was good for nothing! Jimena did make an effort, and she told me she'd deposited a little more money for whatever I needed in Mexico. When are you coming back? she asked every time we spoke. Soon, I'd say. Soon. But I didn't want to go back. Suddenly I had everything I'd been missing in Spain: food, grandparents, attention. Normalcy. No asses, no diapers, no strangers' tears. Why would I go back to Madrid? And why are you staying in Mexico? Jimena asked rhetorically, tell me why. To see why. I'll see. But what you're telling me, child, is that I broke my back to pay for your ticket and now you're not returning! No, I'm just saying that I'll let you know.

Before the rosaries were over, I got up the nerve to ask about Ricardo, and soon I heard that he wasn't around, he'd gone north. What for? I asked. You didn't hear? Hear what? Oh, you don't know anything, it's like you're not even from here. What happened to Ricardo? You remember how he had a dog? Yeah, I remember. Well, he killed the watchman with his dog. What?

I'd been infatuated with Ricardo almost my whole preadolescence. We went to the same grade school, and he was a year ahead of me. But then he failed fourth grade and was put in my class.

The teacher didn't like him, he was always pretty disruptive, but I thought he was nice. He'd ask to copy my homework, but he also made me laugh and gave me some of his lunch. Your granny sent you with a ham sandwich *again*? he'd tease, and I'd say yes. My grandmother always, always gave me ham sandwiches. Then, if he felt like it, he'd share some of his lunch, usually cookies or an egg sandwich. And if he had money, he'd buy me a popsicle, the ones that cost fifty cents. Have a popsicle, you're really skinny and you need to eat. My best friend, Ruth, said he liked me, but I thought we were too young for that stuff and I got nervous and told her no, not to say that. Every time I see you, you're always with my girl, Ruth would say to Ricardo like she was kidding, but then she'd end up pulling me away. If you let him buy you popsicles he's going to want to feel you up. You're crazy, he just gives me his leftovers. You play dumb, but you know what's up, Ruth would say. Ricardo is bad, he hits Marcos, he hits Armando. You want to get hit? Oh, but we just talk at school and that's it. If you don't want problems, don't get involved with Ricardo, she insisted. What do you know? Why are you so against Ricardo? My mom is friends with his mom, Ruth said, and my mom knows that his dad is a general and he's hurt people. That's what my mom says: Like father, like son. And she doesn't let me hang out with Ricardo, so you shouldn't either. But I only half-listened to her, and I talked to Ricardo when she wasn't around, and I told Ruth I bought my own popsicles, though it was a lie because my grandmother never gave me money. Ricardo and I went on being friends until the school year ended and he failed again. He switched to a different school then, we still lived in the same housing complex but we stopped talking, until we got to high school and met again at a party at our neighbor Julio's house.

Did you see who showed up at the party? Ruth asked. And I

turned around to look and felt like I was about to have diarrhea. My stomach, always my stomach. Oh, it's Ricardo, I said. He got cuter, Ruth said, and she laughed. I didn't do anything, and he saw me but didn't say hi and went on talking to his friends, and then Ruth went to the bathroom to make out with a boy, and I stayed in the doorway watching people dance. Then Ricardo walked by with another four kids, and they left the house. We're going to the soccer fields, you coming? one of them said to me. And I didn't say yes and I didn't say no, and they left. About fifteen minutes later I grabbed my jacket and went after them.

Ricardo's friends were passing around a cigarette, while he smoked another one by himself. I went over, and he offered me his. So, I'm still your supplier, huh? You bring your ham sandwich? I smiled. You want this or not? he asked. I said no, because if my grandparents smelled cigarettes on me all bets were off. Then why'd you come? he asked. To see you, I said. And his friends all jeered at us, but Ricardo told them to shut up. He motioned for me to go with him to the end of the field, where there was more privacy.

We didn't talk much, but he did tell me he was going to graduate high school and then enlist. After all, that's what my dad wants, and he won't be happy with anything else. But what do you want? I asked. For him to leave me alone. I'm not like my brother, I won't be a cadet, but I can be a grunt, yeah, I can at least aspire to that. But do you *want* to? I insisted. Why not? he replied. I shrugged. Then we kissed. And I didn't want to seem clumsy, or dumb, or inexperienced, so I started to caress his back under his shirt and he let me, like the inexperienced dummy he was. So I kept going. I put my hand down his pants and his honey-colored eyes looked at me in astonishment. He let me do it, though he didn't do anything to me. So I touched him until he came and got semen all over my hand. He apologized, but I told him it was ok. He gave me his baseball cap to wipe my hand on. Then he gave me another kiss, almost out of obligation, and told me he had to go. I said ok and let him leave. The last time I saw him, before he left for boot camp, he was walking toward the grocery store, which was still run by the military then. I was with my grandmother, and she asked if I knew him. I said yes. Well, don't talk to that kid, don't talk to anyone in his family. Why not? Why do you have to question everything? Just don't talk to him, period. Ricardo, who was with his friends, passed us and said hello. Good afternoon, ma'am! How's the little one? Go to hell, my grandmother said, and Ricardo and his friends burst out laughing. Bye, little one, he called to me, and they walked off. I was mad and sad at the same time, and my grandmother turned to me and said she didn't ever want to see me talking to that boy, and I didn't ask why anymore, I just said ok.

How did Ricardo kill a watchman with a dog? I asked my grandmother, feeling something between shock and disgust. How, I was saying on the inside, could *that* Ricardo—the one who'd been *my* Ricardo—do a thing like that? My grandmother said she'd thought my friends had told me: It was big news, it even made the papers. What happened? Well, that kid was bad, you knew that, he was always a lost cause, and with a father like that . . . What could you expect? The guard got some complaints late that night that they were making too much noise partying at Ricardo's house, so he went to ask them to turn down the music, but Ricardo wouldn't do it and just slammed the door in the guard's face. They say the guard was really young and didn't know what he was doing, he had no experience, just needed a job, so he wanted to let it go, he didn't want any problems, but the neighbors kept calling, saying it was his job, that was what they paid him for. So he went back and insisted they had to end the party. Now it wasn't just about turning down the music, but that anyone who didn't live on the base had to leave. I don't know why, but apparently Ricardo was wearing some boxing gloves and he started to threaten and taunt the guard, so the guard said he was going to call the police, and then Ricardo and his buddies laughed and started shoving him into the house. The neighbors came out to see what was going on. The last thing they saw Ricardo do was take off the boxing gloves, still taunting the guard, and then punch him right in the face. All the friends laughing, more music, turned up even louder. And then the neighbors finally did call the police. When they came, they found the guard dead and the furniture all smashed up. The dog had bitten the guard; at least, they say it was the dog's bite that killed him. I was horrified. I can't believe it, was all I said to my grandmother. You never believe anything. And it was true, I didn't believe in the world, I didn't believe in it exactly as it was. Later that night, I started to laugh and cry—to think that I'd wanted to see Ricardo, who knows what for, but I'd wanted to see him. To tell him about my brother, to find some reason to stay. After hearing about that, I realized I didn't know where my house was. I'd thought that Mexico was my house, and that I could live in it like any mouse.

I GOT THE FEELING that my grandmother wasn't all that surprised by what happened with Diego, as if it had always been his destiny to die that way. What did you expect, that we'd have a Nobel Prize winner in physics born in this house? No, but I didn't expect this. A person is born where they're born and they are what they are, much as your mother may think otherwise. Suddenly my grandmother wasn't my Abuela anymore, no longer the synonym of home, just another woman at the head of a family. My grandmother was no longer the old lady I'd thought about while I bathed Laura in her house in Barcelona, but rather a hard, almost impenetrable woman, like my mother. As if Diego's death had turned her into something else, or as if with my brother's absence and the passage of time, by leaving her house and living far away from her, I had figured out who she really was. As I am now, so you must be, she told me. I didn't know exactly what she meant, but it pissed me off. Did she really want us to normalize Diego's death?

So now you know about Joana, she said, and you know a lot of things about our own family. Diego wanted to defy god and had to meet his wrath. Oh, I really felt like strangling her then. You don't know what it was like in Madrid, Abuela. No, but I do know that you have to face life, you can't run away from it. How do you think I feel when I sit across from Joana's mom or Ruth's mom and tell them my grandson killed himself? What they wouldn't give for their daughters to have had the chance to go on living! Diego was very ungrateful. You always spoiled him. In that last sentence I felt her hatred and resentment toward me. I didn't say anything, not because I believed Diego's suicide was really my fault, but because at that moment a yawning rift opened between her and me. We were no longer grandmother and granddaughter; that whole fantasy of the family that I'd dreamed up in Spain was gone.

My grandfather, though, seemed despondent. Quieter now, no energy. What are we going to do with poor Diego? he asked me, his voice cracking as he stared at the box of ashes. What do you want to do? I asked. How did he seem the last time you saw him? Wasn't he happy? How could this happen out of the blue? I don't think it happened out of the blue, sometimes I think he planned it out, that he'd been saying goodbye to us for a long time and we didn't hear him; but to my grandfather I just shrugged and said nothing. He only shook his head and rested his hands on the box of ashes, as though struggling to understand. I had them make an urn with a cross on the front, I know you don't believe, but . . . It's ok, it's ok, I told him. Didn't he like Madrid? I twisted up my mouth in a gesture of "no." What did those damned Spaniards do to him? he kept on asking, but I didn't know what to say. I didn't know how to express anything. Anyway, what would've happened here? You think he would have stuck around if he was here? That was the only thing I could come up with to say, as though I were defending Madrid. My grandfather pressed his lips together and then sucked in air and ran a hand over my head. Come with me, he said, then picked up the ashes and put them in a backpack. We left the house while my grandmother was at mass.

M Y GRANDFATHER TOOK a big handful from the box of Diego's ashes and put it into a plastic bag that he handed to me. Once again I was touching Diego, soft, fine, almost imperceptible as he sifted through my fingers. We went to pick up the urn that would contain my brother's remains. Very formal, varnished, dark green. Then we headed to the airport and got out of the taxi between the Hangares and Terminal Aérea metro stations. My grandfather led me to the nearest pedestrian bridge, and once we were standing on it he asked me to hand him the plastic bag. And then, just like that, his eyes downcast, a little haltingly, he asked me: What song could we sing for Diego? I looked at him incredulously, but also scared, scared of being just as clumsy as he looked standing there before me. His favorite song? I asked. Yes, one of those songs he used to listen to with you. And I went totally blank: I don't know, Abuelo, they're all in English. Well, in English then, he said expectantly, as though he were ready to start the ritual and I was failing him: *I feel it in my bones, I'm stronger now, I'm ready for the house, such a modest mouse, I can't do it alone, I can't do it alone*, I started to sing out of inertia, mechanically, so as not to ruin the moment. And he poured out Diego's ashes and let them scatter over Mexico City. The place where Diego was born, where I was born, where my mother and grandparents were born. It was our funeral for him, the one most worthy of my brother, or at least that's what I want to believe. Before we left, my grandfather placed some flowers on the bridge. That was where he'd stood and watched us leave for Madrid. And it was there that my grandfather wanted to go, without a word to my grandmother, and cry for Diego, because it seems that we copy ourselves and repeat the same patterns—I guess that's what being a family is. Or that's what I cling to when I think about the family I was once a part of.

I STOPPED ASKING questions about Joana, but I did go and look for Ruth's family. I asked my uncle where her brother was stationed, and it turned out he was in the Defense Department. So I asked my grandfather to call me a trustworthy taxi and I went to find him. It wasn't easy, but I finally got a response when I asked at the hospital entrance. They wanted to know why I was looking for him, and I said I was his girlfriend. And so they walkie-talkied around and summoned him down to the entrance where I was waiting.

When he saw me, his eyes opened wide—he wasn't expecting me. He bought me a coffee inside, since he wasn't allowed to go out in uniform. Things are pretty fucked around here, he told me. It's good you left. He asked why I wanted to know about Ruth, and I said it was impossible for me *not* to want to know about her. Ruth told me you stopped writing her after you left, her brother reproached me, as though feeling out whether I really deserved to know what happened. I admitted it. I was mad, things have been tough, I said. He just smiled. Tough, huh? he asked, toying with a set of keys. What happened to Ruth? I asked. Why don't you just hold on to the idea you have of her? Because she's my friend, you know that. And he did know, she and I had spent almost all of grade school and high school together, we slept over at each other's houses, even spent Christmases together, especially after my mom left for Spain. They were like my second family.

What I can tell you about Ruth is that we would rather leave it alone. It'd be better if you didn't want to know, because the truth is unbearable, he told me seriously. But why? What happened? I kept asking.

Ruth started seeing Joaquín. Joaquín was one of the few guys who got into the Military Academy. Remember? So then we were just waiting for him to get his assignment before they told us Ruth was going with him, and that's what happened. They didn't get married, but Ruth quit school and left with Joaquín. They had to deal with the roughest stuff, it was during the time when there were all those shootouts. Remember? Joaquín was always out on a mission, you know how it goes. Ruth had gone off with him just so she could spend all her time alone. My mom kept telling her to come back, saying she could go visit him every fifteen days, since that's how often she saw him anyway, but they were both crazy about each other, you know how Ruth was. So she stayed there and the shooting started. The ambushes... By then Ruth was only sending us messages, she was always lying flat on the floor, she even saw grenades in the street outside her house. She was really on edge. They lived out by the river crossing where the guys would meet up, you know? And then, who knows what Joaquín got mixed up in, but they came for him and some others from his detachment. They were ambushed in a bar, right there with civilians all around, and kids. This was one of those rural places, you know, where they sell tacos and beer, carnita asada and all that. My sister and Joaquín went there for dinner that night with some other, lower-rank soldiers, and that's where they got hit. They all died. Joaquín was the only cadet there, and the news didn't even say they were military, just that there were such and such many deaths. There were like seven of them, plus my sister and another eight who had nothing to do with it, who were just there to eat. Ruth's body was destroyed, they gave it back to us practically in pieces, in plastic bags, because they were up to their ears in bodies. My dad and I went to pick her up. You can't imagine what it's like to bring your sister or your brother-in-law home like that, in those conditions. But that's what happened, and that's how it was, or is, it's just that we practically don't talk about this anymore—what's the point? It's just more propaganda for those fuckers. But that's what happened to Ruth. She went north to die.

But what did Joaquín do? I asked. Who knows. People say things, but what good does knowing do? Will it bring my sister back? It'll just make them more likely to keep tabs on us, to find out who we are, because there are moles everywhere. Why find out? If Joaquín did things he shouldn't have, that's between him and god, and him and my sister. Around here, we're just sticking with the idea that it shouldn't have gone down like that, but at least they went together. Imagine Ruth spending her whole life crying over Joaquín. No . . . I mean, no, right? Right, I said, just to say something.

Later, we made plans to see each other again at his house, so I could visit his mom and meet his older brother's kids. His mom took care of them: little twins, a boy and a girl, and the girl was named Ruth, obviously. He asked for my phone number, and we even took some photos together. But he never called.

Ruth died very young; she, Diego, and Joana were all very young. I was left alone, ever more alone.

I DIDN'T KNOW if it made sense to tell my grandfather the things Diego did in Madrid or not. I didn't want to change his idea of my brother, but he insisted he wanted to know what happened. I don't know what he did, Abuelo, really, because by then I was in Barcelona, but I do know he stole money, from Mom and from me. If he did other stuff I don't know about it, because I didn't see it and Mom never told me much.

If you ask me what he did, or what he did to me, well, he made me grow up all at once. It caught me off guard, one day he was a little boy who obeyed and respected me, and the next day he was an unbearable jerk. He was one of two extremes, and it was hard to deal with him. I will never forget the first time he ran away from home. The memory of it makes me feel like crying: he got mad about some random thing, he and Mom started screaming at each other, and I wanted to stop him from leaving but he shoved me so hard I almost fell over. Then I tried to take his keys away, but by then he was bigger and taller than me and I couldn't. He left me there talking to myself. I remember all it took was the sound of the door closing and my stomach did a somersault. Seeing Diego leave, seeing him lose all respect for us, made me feel like throwing up. As if he had done the worst thing in the world, as if his rebellion had violated something deep under the surface. That's what it really did feel like for me. I went to lie down in bed and think about what to do and I felt as though something had been taken from me, as if Diego had stolen Diego away. Then my mom came in to yell at me, I don't even remember exactly why, but I won't ever forget her blue dress with its blue buttons, Smurf-colored, as she told me all about how Diego and I were the same, how we only ever brought her problems and never solutions, and she told me to do something: Go out and look for him, bring him home, I'm about ready to send you both back to Mexico! And I almost never talked back to my mom because I knew that no matter what I said to her, she would always be able to twist things and make everything into her own problem, as if the very fact of our breathing, our being born, our living, eating, shitting, each and every thing we did was something we did *to her*, just to hurt her, as if we were spiteful and we hated her. All she did was yell at me, and I put on my coat and went out to look for Diego at La Vaguada, in the park, at La Pirámide, all up and down Avenida Monforte de Lemos, but nothing, no sign of Diego. Then I called Marina's mom and Marina's mom called other moms and everyone was asking about Diego, and then Marina's friends added me to WhatsApp groups and sent messages saying that anyone who'd heard from Diego should speak up, that we were worried about him, but no one said anything, no one had heard from him. Then it was midnight and Diego still wasn't answering his phone or messages. I asked Marina to check social media to see if he had posted, but she said no, she couldn't see his profiles because he'd blocked her. And I was scared for Diego to be walking the streets alone because the police had stopped him and asked to see his ID two or three times already, and Diego, who was easily angered, refused to show them his residence card, and the cops loaded him into their patrol car and threatened to deport him, but then they looked more closely and saw he was a minor and then they did call me, but each time they also told me to be careful because we could have easily doctored his papers to make it look like he was a minor, and the next time my brother caused problems they were going to administer biological tests to determine his real age. This isn't like your country, we respect the rules around here. And there I was choking back my rage, but I said yeah, yeah, and they let him go and told him to cut his hair, to think about his appearance, and Diego started to say something smartass, but I told him to zip it and took him home. That's why that time he ran away, I got really worried once the sun went down: What if someone sees him out walking alone and takes him to the police station and he's too stubborn to call us and he gets deported? I was afraid of all that happening, and that's why I kept sending messages pleading with him to answer me and let me know he was ok, but he didn't answer and I felt like I really had lost him and I wanted to crack open his head and check the neuronal connections and ask him: Where are you? Where did you go, Diego? And he didn't come back that night and I had such a parched mouth and my mom suffered in her own way, and we both went to work the next day, her to take care of the lady who treated her like dirt and me to watch the baby over in Mirasierra and to clean the house, because that couple didn't think I had enough work with feeding the baby and keeping it calm, they thought that for ten euros an hour they had the right to ask me to wash clothes, do dishes, and cook food. It's hard for me to get it all done, tía, while I'm taking care of Santi, the woman told me, and she handed him to me while she put on her sneakers and perfume, and then she handed me the list of things to clean. And that day, with my nerves shot and my stomach in my throat, without letting the couple know I was going out with their son, I got on the metro carrying the baby and the diaper bag and I went to Diego's school, which was about three stops away, and I asked about my brother at the front office and they told me he was there but couldn't leave class, and as soon as I heard that the dumbass wasn't such a dumbass, because at least he had gone to school, I felt my soul return to my body, and I felt less dread as I cradled the baby and took him to walk around La Vaguada until Diego got out, because I wanted to be there before he got the idea to slip away again, and there I was carrying the restless baby up the stairs to the building's main entrance to catch him. And that's how it was, the moment we saw each other the anger went to our heads—dark, dark heads, but the blood in our faces was evident. He didn't say hi or anything, just let me walk next to him, and I asked him what was in that head of his, and he said, Shit, he was sure he had shit in his head, and I made a gesture of fuck-you-you-fucking-asshole pendejo and asked him what he thought he was going to do, and the little jerk was all, Nothing, same as always, I'm going home. And me: Just like that? You have us scared shitless and now you're saying it's all good, all cool, you're just heading home . . . And him, still stubborn as hell and all cocky: I'm not gonna apologize, don't even ask. You already stuck your nose in and now the whole school knows and I had to sit there listening to the fucking guidance counselor tell me how that's not the way things are done and give me her little morality lessons. I'm not gonna apologize, that little shit told me, and there I'd been with my stomach a mess, up all night with diarrhea, the pit of my stomach on fire. I'm not sorry, I'd had it up to my balls with you two, he told me, and I felt like slapping him. It all seemed so harsh and my blood was boiling, but at the same time I was so scared of saying anything that would make him leave again and disappear for good this time, and so I held back, held it all back, I stopped myself from saying anything, from moving any differently. I just walked home with him to be sure he went into the apartment and into his room, and I still had the baby, who was hungry by then, so I gave him a banana from the kitchen and changed his diaper and soothed him, trembling all over from that noxious fear that Diego would leave again, but he stayed in his room with the door closed, and I had to take a deep breath and fight back the urge to lock him in the house, to take away his keys, to beg him please not to go, not to do this to me again. And then I went to return the baby and finish making everything nice for when his parents got home, so they could take off their shoes and get the place dirty again, because then I'd be back to clean it all.

WHEN RICARDO RETURNED from basic training, we started dating in secret. Though it would be an exaggeration to say I was his girlfriend, because really, I wasn't. We only saw each other for a little while whenever he had a day off. And it's not like we talked much, either—Ricardo wasn't really one for talking. We saw each other at the detachment inside the base, because although at first he was stationed at Santa Lucía, he came back to visit his buddies, or else to do things I never found out about. And we'd sneak off into the bushes in the backyard to make out, and we went on that way for about three months. Then they made him a guard at the military bank right there on the base, and that was good because his schedule was one day on, one day off, and on his day off we made the most of his guardsman's bed, while his buddies kept watch for us.

All that hiding, keeping secret the fact that I was seeing him in spite of the warnings from my friends and family—it made me feel alive. He'd buy me a little something and then we'd fuck. That first time I really was turned on, and he whispered into my ear about how much he'd wanted to do that with me. And I let him do it, and since it was the first time I thought it was all great, but after that it wasn't so nice anymore. It seemed like Ricardo was always someplace else, he kissed me and touched me and even looked right into my eyes, but he didn't see me, his eyes

were always absent, and I tried my best to believe he was thinking about me and that I was important to him, but the truth is I
was always the one to seek him out and the one who wanted to
meet up. Ricardo was always someplace else.

One day, my grandparents went to the basilica and left us
home alone. They went out early and told me I would have to
cook for myself and Diego, that they'd be back late. I said ok,
and as soon as I saw them walk out and close the door, I ran
to call Ricardo, telling him to come over right then, because
Diego was still asleep. And he did, he got there fast because
everything was close by, and we went into the bathroom. And
just like that, without warning, he pushed me up against the
sink and finished fast, but I didn't finish. So I told him to do
it again, that I wanted more, and he laughed, but he liked it
and told me to give him a second and he started to touch himself so he'd get hard again, and I said: Let me help, and I bent
down to suck his dick. And my efforts were starting to pay off
when I opened my eyes and saw Diego peeking in through
the door that was open a crack. I slammed it in his face and
leapt to my feet and Diego started crying from the fright and
I told Ricardo to leave. It took me a long time to soothe my
brother and make him understand things in a different way so
he wouldn't tell on me to our grandparents. What you saw was
a dream, Diego, there was no one in the house when you woke
up. Yes, there was a guy, and you were sucking on his pipi. Oh,
Diego, no, that's so gross! And Diego got scared again and
started to cry. And we went on like that for a good while until
I convinced him that he'd been the one who had misbehaved
and that since he had done something very bad, he couldn't tell
our grandparents. What you think you saw is horrible, Diego,
and if you tell them they're going to ground you from watch-

ing TV, I said. And that was what kept him from telling on me, although when he was a little older, one day, out of the blue, in the bathtub while he was rinsing off and I was watching him, he touched his penis and turned to me and said very seriously: One time you sucked on a boy's pipi, right?

I DIDN'T BREAK UP with Ricardo, because we didn't have a relationship. But I stopped seeking him out after I saw him walking and laughing with Ana, one of our grade-school classmates. I felt it like a punch to the gut, but I hid it well and so did he. He saw me go right past them and shoot him an evil glare, but he just kept walking all nonchalantly. I couldn't tell anyone I was sad, because no one even knew we were seeing each other.

But I did start to hate Ana. I didn't want to see her or run into her on the street. That was the first time I really felt like leaving Mexico and convincing Mom to let us live with her. The neighborhood started to feel small: always the same people, always the same things, always isolated from the rest of the world, always around military families, always in a little bubble. Always seeing the same people go away, then come back; first Ruth's family was being sent to Sinaloa or Durango—and in the middle of the school year, we grumbled—then they'd come back after six months, then they would leave again. I was one of the few who didn't move around, because my grandfather was already retired, but the others, the others were always coming and going. They always came back—what a drag.

And Ana's family was more or less like mine, stable, because her mom was a military doctor; they lived in the other housing complex across from ours, where the higher-ups had their homes and their park. Not just apartment buildings, but houses with yards, where the generals had their smaller houses, their second families. Still, most of us went to the same school through elementary and high school. That's why it was significant when Ana was moved out of our class and into a private school; it put distance between us. That's what happened.

Ana sat beside me in third grade, and we were friends. We spent recesses with Ruth and Celia, but things were different between Ana and me; sometimes she invited me over for dinner. That was where I learned the order of silverware and about first and second courses. It was also there that I first felt jealous that a girl my age could have a room and toys all to herself.

Sometimes we played actresses, and she would lend me her clothes. Her dresses. And we would do each other's hair and she'd say, Wow, yours is so long, but for some reason I didn't feel like she meant it as a compliment, but rather an observation, as though to document a fact for the record. And one time we happened to take our dresses off at the same time and we were in our underwear and she told me: You always wear the same polka-dot undies. And instead of saying, No, that's not true, I said nothing and got dressed fast so she would stop looking at me. And after that, every time I went to her house I made sure not to wear that underwear, because I felt like if I did, it was a bad thing.

Then it was the end of the year and she wouldn't stop talking about how she wasn't coming back to our school, how her mom was sending her to a different one, and that it was much better, always so much better. Ana, we heard you the first time, Ruth would tell her, but Ana kept it up: My new school has a pool and we get swimming lessons twice a week and they give us five hours of English classes, with teachers who really know English. But even with all they could teach her at her new school, Ana wasn't one of the best students at ours, and when she invited me over it was almost always so we could do our homework together first: If you don't tell me I have everything right, then I can't play with you. And I helped her, not because she gave me an ultimatum, but because I thought that's what friends did.

That graduation, while we were in line to dance at the end-of-semester recital, Eleonora, another classmate, told me the teacher had said I should go first. I said no. No way! I'm not going first, I told her. Yes, you are, the teacher says you have to go first because you're getting a certificate. A certificate? asked Ana. Yeah, you have to go first now, Eleonora insisted. I started fixing my bun because I thought it was coming undone, and suddenly I felt Ana lifting up my skirt. Look, she's wearing her polka-dot undies again, the ones she always wears, she doesn't have any others, she must not ever wash them! And everyone laughed. I just walked away and went to the front and heard the laughter behind me, and then I heard the teacher's voice calling my name and I was picking up my certificate and Ana and the other kids were behind me, still laughing.

I never talked to Ricardo again after I saw him with Ana, and I felt the whole thing like some kind of double betrayal. That was when I started pressuring Diego to tell Mom she had to come and get us. Tell her you want to go to Madrid, tell her you're the one who wants to go! And Diego was all, No, no, he wanted to stay with our grandparents. And I was all, Yes, yes, you have to be with your mom, understand, Diego? You need to be with your mother. How can you know what the future has in store for you if you only live in the past? But I don't even know Mom, I want to stay with Abuela and Abuelo! Well, we have to be with Mom, Diego, we have to get out of here!

I DIDN'T SEE my grandmother cry until my grandfather brought home the urn—green, almost military green, with a Christ on the cross—and told her they should take it to church so the priest could bless it. Then my grandmother looked like Abuela again, the pre-Madrid one, and she put on her black clothes and styled her over-treated hair and wore her high heels, though they didn't fit anymore because her feet and ankles were always swollen from diabetes, and she held out her hand to me, like when I was little, and asked me to go with them. No one else went, not my aunts, not my uncles, not my cousins. Just the three of us, my grandparents and me.

I'd thought my grandmother no longer loved Diego because of what he had done, but now I saw her hold the ashes while she sang whatever they sang at mass, and she kneeled and asked me to kneel beside her, and I saw the tears on her face, on her cheeks, on the bags beneath her eyes, on her nose, her runny nose. She was secreting Diego's absence all over, and I remembered my train ride to Madrid and how much I'd cried over Diego, lying, mean, and selfish as he was. But when I was sitting there beside my grandmother in the midst of mourning, I thought differently: Be what you want, Diego, be whatever you feel like being, dream of returning to the ocean, and remain here, in our grandmother's ocean of tears. Be the dead man you wanted to be.

And I didn't cry, I didn't feel like crying. Suddenly, just like that, with my grandparents beside me, I supported what Diego had done, I embraced his decision. There was no full life ahead of us. On the contrary: there were crumbs, loose puzzle pieces, a clock with its progressive tick-tock, and a series of battered events piled one on top of the other and leading in no particular direction. None of that "You've got your whole life ahead of you" bullshit, not for Diego and not for me. At least my brother had the clarity to see it, and to take the risk of being the only one to decide his fate.

I want to know if you care about what's happening to us, I said to my mom before leaving for Mexico with her son. She looked at me, serious, calm, her expression dry and blank, but she didn't say a word. It was Jimena who walked me out to the taxi.

Child, you're carrying your brother there. You grieve your own way, and don't go digging into the suffering of others.

WHEN EZRA KOENIG WROTE *I want to know, does it bother you? / The low click of a ticking clock / There's a headstone right in front of you / And everyone I know,* he wasn't talking about Mexico, or about Diego, but Diego repeated that verse a lot, and listened to the song on repeat: *There's a headstone right in front of you and everyone I know,* he'd intone, in English. What are you saying? Nothing, he'd reply and laugh at how no one understood his joke. He was so successful at using that answer to unsettle anyone who'd listen that he made it into a kind of personal signature. If Diego felt bad: *There's a headstone right in front of you . . .* If Diego felt good: *There's a headstone right in front of you . . .* He even put it as his WhatsApp status. He was obsessed.

I didn't understand it until he killed himself and I went back to Mexico to mourn. Ruth, Joaquín, Joana, Diego . . . So many deaths and we were surprised by each one, as if we didn't know we were all going to die. But there are deaths and then there are deaths. Diego's seemed like the most commendable one to me.

Before going back, before I knew I was going back to Madrid, my grandmother asked me to help her clean her house. I can't pay you in euros, but I will pay you. I rolled my eyes. Her words hurt, but by then we were a couple of mean, wounded little animals just trying to avoid any more bruises, so I didn't react to her bite. We started in the room where she stored all our stuff.

She didn't look at Diego's things, just left them stuffed in the back of the closet, but she did start tossing everything else. Look, your mom's wedding dress. So skinny. Look, your aunt's first communion dress. Look, your uncle's first suit. Look, here's your grandfather, when he was young and came to my house to tell my dad he was taking me with him. In a soldier's uniform? I asked. Of course, in his uniform! Otherwise my father wouldn't have taken him seriously. My dad only let me marry him because he knew that in the army we'd have a guaranteed income. And that's what happened, see, and here we are, thank god. But did you want to, Abuela? Is this where you wanted to be? I thought so, she said. But maybe I could have gone somewhere else. Maybe I could have gotten far away. Where would you have wanted to go? Away from here, that's all, away from here. So much violence, so many bad people. But there are bad people everywhere, Abuela. I know, I know. Look, just look at this junk, I think these are from the '86 World Cup, throw them out, throw them out! And we threw away a lot, almost everything. I kept Diego's rainbow blanket. My grandmother was performing her own ritual there among the garbage bags, without even knowing that things were going to change for us all that very night. As if something inside her was telling her we needed to lighten our load, that we had to learn to go on with nothing, because in front of us, right in front of us and everyone we knew, there were headstones with our names on them.

ECAUSE MY MOM was in a hurry, or maybe because the insurance company or funeral home was, I had to take a flight from Madrid to New York and then New York to Mexico, almost twenty-four hours total with the layover. Several hours spent wandering through the airport. Two and a half hours in the immigration line. There were a lot of us wanting to be the crack in their wall.

My mom had gotten our visas when she went to Spain because she knew these things could happen, urgent flights with stop-overs in the U.S. The United States was always in the middle of our relationship with Mom, especially between her and Diego, because my brother always conflated Spain with the United States, he didn't know the difference. Mom, can you send me those chocolates with faces of superheroes on them? Mom, can you send me that thing from New York that was in that one movie? Mom, when you take me to New York, are we gonna eat hot dogs? And my mother, who thought everything was des-tined for my brother anyway, said yes to everything. After all, if she flew over in a plane every day, how hard could it be to stop by New York and buy a little something for my brother?

In real life it was my grandmother's sister in Houston who sent us things. My grandmother had a lot of family living in the U.S., but not in New York, and anyway, Houston, Dubai, Berlin, what difference did it make? Put chocolate in front of

Diego and tell him it came down from heaven itself, and he would eat it happily.

We'd also had dreams of New York, Diego and me, but our hopes were dashed. In real life, they didn't want to let us in even to get to Mexico. *What are you doing here and where are you going?* Mexico, because that's where I'm from. *Are you spending some time here in the city?* No, no, it's just a layover, I'm going to Mexico. *Are you going to leave the airport?* No, I'll stay here. *With whom will you stay?* No one, I'm going to México. *Are you from Mexico?* Yes, I am. *But do you live in Spain?* Yes, I do. *Where is your ticket back to Spain?* I don't have it printed out, should I look for it on my phone? *Yes, yes, look it up.* And I do, I look up the reservation, the number, I type the confirmation code, try to download the ticket, to show that I can't check in yet. I can't get a boarding pass, but this is it, see? *This is in Spanish . . .* Sí, claro que está en español, carajo, of course it's in Spanish, and there I am changing the version of the airline's website to English because this big fat hijodelachonchadesumadre motherfucker can put me through this, just because he wants to, oh yes, he wants to and he can. The Spanish couple who went before me didn't have to do any of this shit, and no one asked them to speak so much English, or asked them why they knew English, or was surprised that they could answer in English, or sat staring at the pinche photographs on their passports and visas like it was a fucking fake ticket, no, no, they just checked their information, end of story; because New York, Madrid, Barcelona, they're all the same, you know, tíos, como en los erizos.

But I got through, and I wandered down all the halls with all the fucking stores full of large and extra-large products that I was now allowed access to after their gringo police had inspected me, because why not.

What bothers you so much about that? It's their job! Tom-Tomás asked me once, and I just looked at him with my oh-you're-a-real-dumbass expression, because I wasn't about to explain that asshole's pinche racism, nor was I going to explain exactly why he was a dumbass. I get mad because I get mad. Yeah, but . . . But nothing, just shut up, will you? And he laughed. Tom-Tomás never seemed more like a pendejo idiot culero asshole than when I was wandering the halls of the New York airport. But Diego and I were bigger pendejos: Oh, yeah, when we go to New York and buy our Cake Boss, when we buy real Dunkin' Donuts, and when we tour Manhattan and become J. Lo's heirs or something, oh, yes, Diego, how happy we'll be then, we'll have such a good time, far away from Mom and from the new life and the old life, it'll be another life, Diego, not the one we were born into, not the one that was forced on us, not the one we fled, but *our* life, the one we choose for ourselves, here in New York, buying things, consuming things, letting the gringos really believe they're the greatest, just la hostia, that they really are the most chingones, just look at everyone wanting to live in New York, which has rats, which has bedbugs, which has raccoon infestations, which is more expensive than Madrid or Barcelona, where it's this and that and the other, yes, Diego, how happy we'll be once we're in New York and we speak English with the English speakers, but also so they won't tell us to go back to our country because 'We speak English around here,' so they won't stick a phone camera in front of us and tell us to leave, so we don't get all mad and offended then and tell them, oh, yeah, fucking redneck, oh, sure, pinche gilipollas, oh yeah, we all hate each other, but how happy we're going to be in New York, Diego, and we're going to go to all the places we want to see because, no matter how much you sing your Vampire Weekend, they're not singing to you, they don't know anything about you and they don't want to, they're not interested in learning a thing about you, they don't know that those four albums and all their songs were the only thing you left in your pinche phone for me to remember you by. How happy we'll be, Diego, in New York! But I was thinking all of that by myself, as I was taking my brother to Mexico in a little wooden box, certified, evaluated, and thoroughly approved by the immigration authorities, both in Spain and in Niuyor.

I F I COULDN'T believe in Diego, who could I believe in? I couldn't see a future, or an answer to my own life, or to why it is that some plants move and that we, so self-absorbed, don't notice and let them die, believing that the only thing they were good for was to adorn the very idea that they help us breathe. I no longer believed in the promise of the euro, or the dollar, or the peso. If I couldn't believe in Diego, who could I believe in?

M Y GRANDMOTHER ALWAYS taught us to respect plants. We grew up in a house full of them, especially the climbing vines and ivies that encased the whole place. It looks like a jungle, Diego would say, jumping from sofa to sofa and shouting like Tarzan. But god help him if he jumped wrong and fell onto one of our grandmother's flowerpots—then there was no gap-toothed grin or big sister in the world who could assuage her fury. Not the plants, not the plants! And my grandmother talked and sang to them, same as when she made tamales and talked to the dough so it wouldn't separate, so the tamales would turn out nice and spongey. After all, it's still corn, it's a plant, it can hear you and it knows what it's here for, she told us, and Diego and I held back our laughter, but we listened to her. Do plants really move? my brother asked me, staring hard at them, and I said: Yes, they really do, and when he least expected it, I'd shake a flowerpot or something and say, Watch out, Diego, the plant is moving, it's gonna eat you!

The night my grandmother asked me to help take out all the garbage bags filled with stuff from our old room, I carried the biggest ones out to the sidewalk first, hoping the night watchman would see them and take them to people who could use those things. But I didn't see the guard, I just saw several cars speeding down our street, headed toward the entrance to the base. The atmosphere felt strange, as if our building were echoing with some far-off, murmuring voice. That was all I saw: a lot of cars and pickups and a weird atmosphere, almost no one out in the street.

Then I went to take a shower, so I didn't hear the phone ring or my grandfather talking to someone. Nor did I hear my grandmother shout: Oh my god! I came out nonchalantly to see what was for dinner and I called to my grandfather from the kitchen that we were out of the hot sauce I liked and asked if I could run to the store for some more. I got no response. I went to look for them in their room, and the door was closed. Abuela? Abuelo? And the phone rang again. They both came out practically running, fighting over who would answer. What time did you talk to him last? Where is he now? Don't come, don't come! My grandmother brought her hands to her chest and my grandfather hung up with his eyes fixed on the window. What's wrong, Abuelo? He didn't look at me. Call Carmela, keep trying her, he ordered my grandmother.

Carmela was my aunt, my mom's younger sister. She lived on the base too, but farther down, near the soccer fields and basketball courts where I met up with Ricardo that first time. Her husband was a second sergeant; my uncle and grandfather had pulled strings to get an apartment rental for them there, because second sergeants didn't get apartments. My grandmother called Aunt Carmela. No one answered, so my grandfather put on his sweater and said he was going out to look for her. My grandmother said ok and started dialing again to see if she'd have better luck. She didn't. My grandfather left. I watched him from the window, feeling very afraid. I crossed my fingers, like for good luck. Hold us in your everlasting arms, my grandmother said, my god, almighty god, hold us in your glory. And she carried a candle into Diego's room and set it on the table with my brother's ashes and photo. The flame lit up his ten-year-old face, and I thought that whatever this was, Diego wasn't going to help us.

What's wrong, Abuela? But my grandmother gave me nothing. You just stay calm, we're going to figure this out. But, what's wrong? What's going on with Aunt Carmela? We can't find her! What about her kids? Them either! And with that habit of hers of always needing to do something, she started to mechanically water the plants, turning toward the window every time it lit up with the headlights of the cars that were still driving around.

But who was it on the phone, Abuela? You have to tell me. But she wouldn't tell me a thing. Don't get in the way, learn to listen and keep quiet, she said, and so we sat there, wordlessly avoiding each other's eyes, until my grandfather came in with a look that I'd never seen before and said: Don't leave the house, something's happening, I don't know what it is, but don't go out, I'll be right back. But I jumped up from the sofa: No! You're not going alone, I'm coming with you. My grandmother shouted something at me but I was already putting on my jacket. I grabbed his hand and followed him. The last thing I heard was my grandmother asking where Aunt Carmela could be, but still, no one knew a thing.

MY GRANDFATHER, who was skinny and bony but tall and sure-footed, had his head down and his back hunched while we walked. Where are we going, Abuelo? I asked. But he just kept walking, holding my hand tight. The street was empty as if everyone was hiding, but in the distance, right at the entrance to the base, I heard noise. I thought we were headed there, but then my grandfather turned toward Ricardo's parents' place. We didn't get as far as his apartment, which was 302. We stayed in the entryway, where someone had hung a white sheet with red letters that said: Come out and you'll lose your head.

I think I screamed in silence, if that's possible—as if I heard myself scream and covered my own mouth before it could be heard by anyone else. The street lamp was the only light on; all the windows in the buildings were dark. I thought I saw someone on the top floor look out at us, but it was just a curtain moving. I guess my grandfather had gotten his answer, and now he did turn and walk toward the main road. We were headed to the main entrance. Why are we here? I asked. If your buddy Ricardo's dad is fighting for control of the plaza, I figured they'd come here, he said. But I didn't think things had gotten this bad. I swallowed hard. We kept walking and it was as though we were floating, waiting for something more. And we got it: there was a commotion at the base's entrance, where a bunch of people were looking out toward the avenue—specifically, at the bridge over the avenue. No one went out, they were all crowded together, pressed against one another as though protecting themselves and their territory. I saw my ex-classmate Eleonora standing beside her mom, both of them seemingly hypnotized, staring up at the sky. My grandfather and I went out and got as close as we could. I looked up. There, hanging from the pedestrian bridge, were more than ten decapitated bodies. Two cop cars were diverting traffic, and there was nothing else but fear. Call your aunt, keep trying her. I pressed the phone with trembling fingers. Tell me if she answers, he demanded. She didn't answer.

W E NEVER HEARD from my aunt Carmela and her two kids again. That morning, the three of us sat waiting for her husband to call—he was the one who'd warned my uncle, my grandparents' oldest, that something was going down. Carmela's husband never called, though, it was my uncle who did. Apparently, it was all a settling of scores, and they had taken a lot of people, onlookers who happened to be there, innocent bystanders, and the families of the military men involved. None of that was in the news—they just talked about ten decapitated bodies, and everyone assumed they were linked to organized crime. All those bodies were actually military, but no one said that, and really, not much more was said about it at all.

My grandmother told me I had to leave right away: Go back to Madrid, now, you can't stay here. My grandfather agreed: Leave, you have to get out while you can. My uncle warned me that we were all in danger, that my grandparents were going to have to get out too. We left that same morning for his house in the State of Mexico. He asked us to only take what was essential. I took my suitcase and Diego's ashes. My grandparents didn't pack much either, just shut off the electricity and the boiler, threw away the food in the fridge, and, carrying three large black plastic bags, we left the house where my brother and I had been born. I never went back. I left that house without understanding a thing. My grandparents never went back either, they died without ever returning home.

DIEGO HAD FALLEN head over heels for Marina. It was instantaneous. He had never seen a girl like her. And she, for some reason, fell for him too—maybe she'd never seen anyone like him. They dated for a few months, but Marina's parents demanded that she stop seeing him, and their insistence was stronger than any of Diego's efforts to please that family. I left for Barcelona right as their relationship was definitively ending.

I'm not really sure what Diego did to offend them, but I do know that he buckled down to get good grades and do everything that's asked of a high-school kid. They just didn't like him—he went to their house twice, but the second time they wouldn't even let him in, and they told Marina not to go out with him anymore. Marina obeyed them, but at school she acted like Diego's girlfriend. Then Diego started bringing Marina over to our house, and that's how I met her. They saw each other at our place.

I didn't like her or dislike her: I was glad Diego was happy, but I was also nervous to see him so stressed over becoming a person he didn't want to be. Nor did I like that as soon as Marina found out that I was a nanny and cleaned houses and didn't aspire to do anything else, she looked at me differently, and I guess at Diego too, and then he had pressure to be the one to go to college coming at him from all sides. But there would be no college diploma for Diego, or even a high school one. Diego told us all to go to hell.

What I told Diego was that ok, even if Marina did have a better place, a nicer apartment, it's not like she was rich or out of his league. If she lives around here, she's not exactly upper class, I said. But Diego told me I didn't understand and that he wasn't going to explain. Then I took it personally, and it was me against Marina's family, and Marina's family just ignoring us.

Then Marina and Diego fought, and that was when my brother got angry at life. His whole outlook changed. They got back together in the following days, but it wasn't the same anymore, and they yelled at each other. Both of them yelled, but Diego was louder. I stopped him maybe four times: Hold it right there, buddy, you don't talk to anyone like that. He apologized the first time, but after that he told me off, too. Fuck off, this is none of your business, pinche metiche! And then we fought, and that jerk had to fight double-time: with his girlfriend and with me. Those were some rough days for him. I didn't hold back: Diego could be anything he wanted to be, but not an abusive boyfriend. Not that.

Our grandfather never hit us; our grandmother, when we were little, gave us two or three swats, and one time she smacked me and another time she hit me hard. My uncle, Mom's older brother, beat his wife, Margarita, constantly. He had a short fuse, and he'd yell at her and their kids viciously, and I mean viciously. One time he flew off the handle and cornered her, left her cowering against the wall, bleeding. Margarita took the kids to her parents' house. My uncle went to get her, she didn't want to go back, but her parents and my grandparents defended my uncle. My uncle went on hitting her, and my aunt Margarita didn't report him or say anything after that—why would she, when no one would ever back her up?

It happened with my aunt Carmela, too: so pretty and always

dolled up, but still, her husband hit her several times. Once, it was because he read a message from a male friend on her phone. Nothing bad, but my uncle threw a fit and they had an awful fight. My aunt was holding her second baby in her arms, and the guy still kicked her and threw her to the ground, making the baby cry. Another time, my aunt screamed for help and made it far enough to knock on her neighbors' doors; the neighbors didn't let her in, but they were there, listening. So Aunt Carmela left the house barefoot with the baby and her three-year-old daughter and no money at all. She was really scared, but my grandparents didn't say anything, they just let her in, didn't even ask if she was ok physically. And my aunt was a wreck—her mood and her battered face told the same story. Then, the next day, they chewed her out—I remember it well, I was there. My aunt was crying in the bath, and my grandmother went in to berate her. Said she couldn't go around starting drama like that. My aunt couldn't even bring herself to get dressed, she just stood there, naked, while the two of them scolded her, saying she had to get her head on straight or something like that. I had my hands full watching her kids and Diego, but I was still upset about it. My aunt had to go back to her house, and I remember how much it hurt to watch her go, all downcast with one eye still black. I told my mom about it. Mom got mad at my grandparents, and that was when she left home the first time.

That's why I told Diego that I would have none of his hitting and shouting, fuck all that shit, and he told me: Fuck all *your* shit, it's none of your fucking business, pinche metiche culera. Fucking asshole, no wonder they call you Cule at school, I told him. Fucking brat, you don't even know how to wash your own ass yet and here you are thinking you can be a big dick, I told him. Fucking culero, we do *not* hit in this house, I told him.

THEN, DURING THAT TIME WITH MARINA, there was the wooden bat incident. Diego was walking with Marina outside Mom's apartment building in Madrid, and some guys came up behind them yelling and waving a baseball bat. Marina and Diego just wanted to get inside. Right by the building's entrance, there was a bench where the neighbors would meet up to talk and smoke in the evenings, at the end of the workday. Always the same ones: the woman who lived downstairs, the one from the seventh floor, and two retired men who lived in the building, I didn't know exactly where. They all saw that those kids were harassing Diego and that Marina was scared, but they ignored it. When he tried to get into the building, Diego was cut off by another neighbor who was also going in, and who asked them where they were going. Diego replied that he lived there. The neighbors knew him, but they didn't say a word to back him up. The man wouldn't let him in. Then that man joined in with the kids, and they all circled Diego and Marina. Where are you from? they asked my brother. I live here, Diego said. I'm asking where you're *from*, the man insisted. Marina told him that they lived there and to let them through. But the man slammed the door and said no, not until Diego showed them his ID and proved that he lived there. Diego got mad and started shouting that he *did* live there, and all of them, the kids with the baseball bat and the neighbors and others who were crowding around to get a look, they all started telling him to calm down, that there was no need to get aggressive. Marina called her parents, and her parents told her to call the police. She did. No one called me. At that point, Diego was still shouting and people were gathering around to see how it would all end, but no one was on Diego's side, or at least no one acted like it. On the contrary: at that moment, Diego was the violent one. Then the police came, and along with Marina's parents, the kids with the bat, and the neighbors, they warned Diego not to get belligerent. Diego was really angry by then, but he just said ok and that all he wanted was to go home. The police followed him to our door and waited for Diego to get his residence card and show it to them. They told him he couldn't go around making scenes and that any violent act could land him in Moratalaz, at the juvenile detention center. Diego said yes, he understood. Everyone else left and things went back to normal, as if nothing had happened. No one questioned anyone else, not even the kids with the bat, who left nonchalantly right before everyone's eyes. Diego broke up with Marina that day and started skipping school and fighting with me and Mom, and eventually he ran away from home that first time. When I couldn't find him, Marina told me what had happened. He's had me blocked on all his social media since that day with the bat, Diego is really mad at everyone, she said. But why didn't you tell me sooner? I don't know, she told me, I'm sorry, I don't know why I didn't.

WHEN DIEGO SANG *I don't wanna live like this, but I don't wanna die*, I didn't understand what he meant until the thing with Aunt Carmela happened. You were so fucking right, Diego, there were so many things you always understood. Because I could play dumb, pretend I understood and keep going, but Diego, he didn't want to keep going. What for? To live in a city that stacked the deck against him and made him feel unwelcome? To go back to our grandparents and join the army? And then what? Blood, blood, blood, blood, and more blood.

To me, leaving Mexico meant fleeing the violence that still ended up annihilating my family. Another kind of violence awaited us in Spain, a kind that was less showy but equally cruel, where they demanded our loyalty while meticulously humiliating us for not being like them.

I HAD NEVER seen my uncle's house before, because my mom didn't like him. They didn't get along, and my mom told me to stay away from his place. And that's what I did for years, though to tell the truth there weren't many chances to visit him, because it was easier for him to come to my grandparents' than vice versa. It took about two and a half hours in traffic to drive to his house, and it was dangerous to go by public transport—people were always getting mugged.

That's why I was so impressed when we got there. It was like a different world. He lived far away from the city in a very big house. My grandparents would be comfortable there, but I knew I wouldn't. I felt disconnected from everything. There was nothing to make me want to stay; to me, at that moment, the only family relationship I could feel less bad about was the one with my mom. With Diego's return to Mexico, my deaths included Ruth, Joana, my aunt, my cousins, Ricardo, and also my grandparents. They all died on me. Because even if no one believes it, there are people who die on you even though they keep breathing and moving right in front of you.

To tell the truth, I never had a problem with my uncle. I'd always been fond of him when I was little, but as we got older, we didn't spend as much time together. For one thing, he was almost never home; at a young age, he'd started specializing in something I was always hazy on, and he spent a lot of time out. I remember, when I was little, watching him pack his bag to go on survival courses: weeks out in god knows where, learning how to survive and win medals. I'll never forget the first time I saw him organizing his rations. This is for the whole week, there won't be anything else, he said, and all I saw were some protein bars and chocolate. Too much sacrifice, I thought. But he packed his knife and his uniform and other things while my grandmother cooked him mole de olla, his favorite dish, and he ate until he was stuffed because he knew things were going to get rough. There was a time when my uncle was in the Presidential Guard. My grandfather was very proud, but not my grandmother. Don't talk about what your uncle is into, don't tell people what he does. You never know.

My grandmother never wanted her kids to go into the military, but it seemed like the logical thing. My grandfather was military, so his sons were too. They inherit the trade, said Ruth's mom. They inherit it, yes, but they also choose it because it's fast money; it costs so much to go to college and find a job, and they can become soldiers with just a high school degree, said my mom. And that's why my uncle joined the army, because he wanted to support himself, to move out of the family home. So one time, after a fight with my grandfather, he went to the Cuatro Caminos station where some soldiers were recruiting, and in the blink of an eye he was enlisted. My grandfather got really mad because he wanted his kids to at least be cadets, not grunts. You're going to be a grunt! And my uncle: Just like you! And my grandfather: Exactly, exactly! But my grandmother was the most mortified, she didn't want grunts or cadets, but something else entirely. And that something else, she wanted it for Diego and me. You two need to study hard, find something else. But she said it more for Diego. She was terrified that Diego would want to join the military: Not him too, no, let him be something else.

There was one time, when my uncle was still single, when they sent him south. He set off with his hair cut high and tight and his clothes very clean. His shirt was blindingly white, brand new. Back then it wasn't dangerous yet to wear a uniform out in public. I remember he gave me thirty pesos and took Diego and me to buy elotes. Then he dropped us off at our front door and left on foot. I don't know if he went away happy, but he was at least hopeful. Then, about three months later, he came back while Diego and I were watching TV. Uncle's home! my brother cried when he heard his customary whistle, and my grandmother dropped her spoon and ran out with Diego to greet him. I'd imagined a scene like the gringo soldiers coming home from war, everyone all crying and happy, but it wasn't like that. Once he was inside, my grandmother looked him over while she fidgeted, touching her fingernails one after another, and Diego asked: What'd you bring me, what'd you bring me? But my uncle didn't bring anything that day, he didn't even bring himself: he was someone else. I don't really know how, but he was different, exhausted and different. His eyes were extinguished, vacant, angry. That's it, angry and dusty. His clothes were still neat, but worn. He was all worn out: his clothes, his gaze, his skinny body.

My grandmother sent me out to buy tortillas and a can of jalapeños: Ask them for pickled carrots, he likes those a lot. I even remember she called my aunt Carmela and invited her and her family to have dinner with us. My aunt brought rotisserie chicken and necks in Valentina sauce, another of my uncle's favorites. My grandmother set to making refried beans and grilled nopal with fresh cheese. And my uncle sat with us and ate, he let us all finish and even chatted with his brother-in-law. But he wasn't the same, he didn't crack jokes or tease anyone, he just nodded and smiled politely. I confirmed it later with my grandmother. You're right, she said, he looks tired, sad. Maybe he was raped and he's sad like my mom, I said. That was the time my grandmother slapped me: she opened her eyes very wide and gave me two slaps, one on each cheek. Then she started washing the dishes and gave me the silent treatment.

I'll never forget the last time I saw my grandparents, because I would rather not have seen them like that, rather not have that image tattooed on my mind. That day, I got mad at Diego. Fucking Diego, you asshole, you bastard! You sent me back to Mexico to see this, to live through this, to endure everything you were running away from. Fucking Diego, you asshole, they called you El Cule and you deserved it. It would have been so easy for me to stay in Barcelona acting like a victim and suffering my own actions, but no, asshole, you make me go pick you up, you make me take you away and bring you here, you make me see my grandparents without their children, make us watch as they're snatched away, and you, you, you, only you have an altar wherever you go.

My flight was a red-eye, so I would land in Madrid at one in the afternoon. Jimena was going to pick me up. I had to be at the airport three hours early, and leave my uncle's house at least three hours before that to get there on time. Six hours just to start the journey. It all felt endless, and so tedious.

Though my grandparents sent me off with a hug and a kiss, I didn't feel them. It was all mechanical. They even smelled different. They were like wet cardboard cutouts, stale crackers, hard meringue. They carried my suitcase to my uncle's car and waved goodbye. The two of them close together but detached. They had broken apart. That's how they looked that last time I saw them, like popsicle sticks glued to poster board and about to fall off. Fucking Diego, I thought, I've gone through all this alone, without you. After I flew back to Madrid, I talked to my grandparents a couple of times on the phone; they were distracted, of course. They died soon after. Without ever finding out where their daughter Carmela and their grandchildren had ended up. My grandfather died in the hospital, of old age, my uncle told us. Then my grandmother, sitting in front of Diego's ashes and the photo of her children. My uncle said she seemed at peace.

THE DAY MY BROTHER AND I left Mexico for Madrid, although we felt sad, we were happy. Sad but happy. We're going to fly! Diego said to me, all excited. I settled in beside him thinking that what I was feeling was the taste of adventure. I picture my uncle headed to the south of Mexico, settling into his seat in the military transport, thinking about how his life was about to do a full one-eighty and smiling innocently at that fact. Years later, it would be him and me settling into his car so he could drive me to the airport on my way back to Madrid. No adventure there. Too much death. If only we'd never taken that fucking one-eighty.

MY UNCLE KNEW that I occasionally ate Diego. He told me he'd seen me do it several times, but he couldn't believe his eyes, and that's why he couldn't bring himself to say anything at the time. Why do you do it? he asked now, as we drove. I was silent. It's bad for you, it'll make you sick. If only, I answered, without reasoning much. If only what? If only you got sick and died? he reproached me. You think you deserve everything because your mom abandoned you and your brother. Poor little you, he said, his voice mocking and angry. In this family, he said, pointing a finger at me, your mother was the only one who was able to shake off all this shit we live in. Quit feeling sorry for yourself and honor her decision. I snorted, again without thinking. He just gave me a dirty look and turned on the radio. He dropped me off at Terminal Two so he wouldn't have to pay for parking. We hugged, but we didn't hug. Over time, I stopped talking to him, too. It was as if after that day, my whole family went silent in honor of their dead. Static, immobile, destined to be scorned, then forgotten.

PART FOUR

I READ ONLINE that the ashes of dead people aren't toxic, and that they're basically just a mix of cellulose, tannins, calcium and potassium salts, carbonate, and phosphate. I never got sick from eating Diego's ashes. The day I went to say goodbye to his altar at my uncle's house, before we left for the airport, I put another handful of him into a plastic bag and packed it in my suitcase with my clothes. I don't know why I ate my brother, but it soothed me. Having his ashes on my tongue, so fine they were almost imperceptible, brought me peace. I don't have an explanation for it, and I'm not going to try to give one. Did I eat his ashes? Yes. Why? I don't know. Does it matter? No. Do I regret it? No. Why not? Because that's the way things are, you do them and that's it. I would have kept doing it, but I ran out. I didn't notice, or I only noticed once all that was left was a dirty baggie. That's how Diego disappeared forever from Madrid, badda-bing, badda-boom, first on the ground, then in a bag. That's how we all disappear.

Y OU WANT TO see the exact spot where Diego fell? No, Mom, I don't want to. There's nothing left of him. I would hope not. But they cleaned. They cleaned it all, as though to erase him quickly. Did you see? I asked. No, I heard about it. Who from? People. So you didn't see it? I saw my son alive at seven in the morning when I left. But did you see him like *that*? I insisted. Had you talked to him in those days? she asked, avoiding the question. I said no.

I did see the exact spot where Diego fell. I spent a long time at the open window looking down and trying to imagine it. I even dropped a few things: a napkin, a coin, a plastic figurine from the bookcase. They all fell differently. Almost soundlessly, even the coin. I didn't feel sad; I felt nothing, in fact. I just stood there looking down, and that was all. It was Jimena who told me to get away from the window. I obeyed. Then, at midnight, when the street was empty, I went downstairs and straight to the place where Mom had been told Diego's body landed. I was afraid at first, but then I knelt and touched the ground. He wasn't there. Even though there were surely minuscule particles of his body embedded in the sidewalk, he wasn't there. There was nothing. Where did he go? At that moment I thought he'd gone to Mexico, but now I really don't know. First, I imagined Diego breaking like a musical instrument, everything splintering, splitting into little wooden pieces with a low boom deep enough to echo all through the neighborhood, his little pieces flying chaotically every which way. But really, I think it's more that I don't want him to crash. I prefer him suspended, not rising or falling, just suspended, eternal in an instant, everywhere and nowhere at once. Like music, which only exists when it's played or sung.

When Diego was little, he used to say that the streetlights looked like lit-up oranges. That night, there were oranges watching over me from atop those streetlamps, but they weren't any kind of sign. There was no magical moment when Diego bade me farewell or convinced me that he was still in this world. I'm just describing events because I can't describe anything else. I don't want to describe anything. What happened happened.

I T WASN'T ALL: evil Diego, bad Diego, oh, how Diego's turned into such a hateful teenage boy. It wasn't like that. Jimena told me how Diego was there the day a family on the second floor got evicted. She told me how the two of them saw the police cars pull up and they watched the whole thing from the window. How they heard the police on the intercom asking the family to open up and the family wouldn't do it, so the cops started calling other apartments. How Diego picked up the receiver and told them to go away. But eventually the family did let them in. Diego and Jimena went down along with another neighbor to see what was going on. There was no resistance: in under two hours, all the family's furniture was out in the street. Jimena gave them water because she couldn't think of anything else, and Diego offered to watch the two little kids while the parents made phone calls and tried to find someplace to go. Diego was there for a good while, taking care of the kids, playing with them. He even gave them some toys he had in his room, and when someone finally came to pick up the family's belongings, Diego sat watching from the window until they were gone. Jimena says that my brother didn't cry, because he could endure a lot, but he did seem really down. Oh, kiddo, don't take it to heart, the world is like that. Like what? he asked, shitty and full of assholes? Well, yes, just like that.

I remember how when Diego was little, he cried over our aunt Carmela and her husband leaving home. The tears he didn't cry for Mom, or for his dad, he cried for my aunt and uncle. Why are they leaving? he asked me with his dark little eyes, his little hands over his face. Oh, Diego, don't cry, they're ok, they're leaving because they have to do their own thing. No, no, I don't want them to go. And I hugged him and tried to make him understand that it wasn't a bad thing to leave. But I don't want them to go, they're leaving their room all alone and the walls will be lonely. The walls? Yeah, the walls. And I imagine Diego thinking about the second-floor apartment, empty, its walls sad, the family leaving in a sort of betrayal of the building and the community, and the child Diego inside teenage Diego saying: Why are they going, why are they leaving the walls all alone? And I was off in Barcelona, not hugging him and unable to tell him that everything was going to be ok, even if it wasn't.

THERE WERE TWENTY-EIGHT STUDENTS in my brother's class. Seventeen were the children of immigrants, four had been born in Madrid, and the rest were Spanish but from other towns. Almost no one rooted for Real Madrid, except for a boy they called Bolivia, who had a Bolivian mom and a Spanish dad. The kids had nicknamed him Bolivia when he was little, even though he spoke with a Madrid accent and had the Real Madrid shield on his backpack. The others were all Barcelona fans, including Diego, and so they teased Bolivia about soccer. Then Bolivia, who had always been the smallest in elementary school, had a growth spurt in high school, and went from being bullied to being a bully. Diego and Moisés were his main targets, because they had the darkest skin. Fucking monkeys, shouldn't you be in the zoo? and he made monkey noises to taunt them. Several times he left bananas on a chair for Moisés, who was Colombian. And when Moisés would pick them up to throw them out or something, Bolivia would start acting like a monkey and everyone laughed. At first Diego didn't say anything, but then he did step in and tell Bolivia not to act like such an asshole. From then on, they were rivals and had it out for each other. The thing is that although Diego didn't really have enemies, he also didn't have many guy friends. He felt more comfortable with the girls in his class, like Marina, than with the boys. Fag! Bolivia yelled at him, and Diego retorted: Go fuck yourself, asshole.

Once, when Bolivia left the usual banana on Moisés's seat, Diego went and ate it, acting like a monkey while he stuffed it in his mouth. Everyone laughed at him, but Bolivia took it as the slap in the face that it was, and a few days later, along with two other classmates, they stole my brother's Language textbook again. The two of them fought. Diego got punished for having eaten the banana, but they never checked to see if the other kids had the Language book. Until one day, Bolivia took out the stolen book, either by mistake or to get under Diego's skin. When Diego saw it, he told Bolivia out loud and in front of the teacher that the book was his, and to give it back. They argued, and the teacher sent them both to the guidance counselor. She gave Diego his book back, made Bolivia apologize, and let them go without even a slap on the wrist. But Diego went at Bolivia and gave him a black eye. The school warned Mom that the next time, my brother would be kicked out of school, and they would report to the police that my brother was violent; they threatened her by saying the police might look into his home life, because it was clear that something was wrong. My mom said yes, ok, to everything. She fought with Diego, she reproached him for even being born, and Diego ran away again. That time he didn't go home for three days, and when he did, he apologized to Mom. Jimena says that they cried a lot that day, and that even though they had some words they were fine in the end, eventually they hugged and made up. My mom says that at the time she didn't understand what Diego was telling her, but that when she found out her son had jumped from the window, she understood everything. He hadn't been apologizing for running away from home, or for making trouble at school. Diego had been apologizing because from then on, he knew he was going to kill himself.

YOU THINK IF I tell Mom I want to be a pilot she'll send me back to Mexico? You want to go back to Mexico? No, but I don't know what I want to do, and I don't have the grades to be a pilot here. How do you know, you looked it up? Yeah, and I don't have the GPA. And in Mexico would you be a military pilot? Hell no, of course not! Would you ever become a soldier, Diego? Maybe here, in Spain, maybe that way they'd give me citizenship and I'd be less of a dead weight for Mom. Still, the *army*? They must be really hard on the people who aren't Spanish, like to prove something; I don't know, but I bet they are. Well, they say that your name is your destiny, he said with a laugh. What do you mean? I mean that Diego is biblical, maybe my destiny is to teach by example. And we both burst out laughing. Don't join the military, I told him. Of course I won't, he replied, what a drag to wrap myself up in a flag while I'm flying.

I DON'T WANT you to leave like this, carrying your brother away and thinking it was all just sadness and pain, Jimena told me before I left for Mexico. There were good things. We weren't the model happy family, but there were good things. I loved your brother, and I think he loved me. And your mom loves both of you. I smiled, to acknowledge her good intentions. Then I said, I told you once that my mother was a burden, and you didn't deny it. What could I say? You're going to have to choose between wanting the mother you think you deserve or accepting the mother you have. What were the good things? I asked. Give me one example. One? Girl, I've got lots! But I'll give you one. And she invited me to eat on Fernández Almagro. Come have lunch with me before you leave. And we went. My mom was at the doctor, because the woman she took care of felt sick and there was no one else to take her. When Mom found out where we were going, she asked Jimena to bring her what her son would have eaten: Order me exactly what Diego used to get! I heard her say over the phone. And Jimena ordered it: half a grilled chicken with French fries to go, with a lot of sauce, the house special sauce. Jimena and I ate chicken, too, Dominican style. You see how small this place is, on weekends it gets full, we always had to call on Thursday to make a reservation. Diego really liked coming here. We brought him on Sundays. Half a chicken for him, with fries and a Coke. He didn't talk much, or look at us, but he was doing a lot just by sitting down and eating with us and letting us talk without interrupting or getting defensive. Take your time there, champ! your mom would tell him when she saw him wolfing down his chicken. Have some more fries! And Diego would laugh and eat more slowly, though that chicken didn't last long with him, and if he was in a good mood he'd ask your mom if he could order more, and your mom would say yes and then give him some of her food. And that brief moment, when they allowed themselves to exchange plates like mother and son—that was a good thing. Sharing a table with Diego every Sunday was a good thing. Yes.

MANY YEARS HAD to pass before Diego and I could go live with Mom in Madrid. Years in which she had to get married so she could have a residence card and not just a work permit, because she never would have gotten residency as a mere caregiver. And so she got married, and she didn't say a word to us, her children, let alone to our grandparents. This guy took pity on her, let's say, but really it was more like he gave her a loan, which my mom spent a long time paying back. Even when we were doing the residency paperwork for Diego and me, my mom had to find him and get him to sign the papers and put in an appearance with his ID the day she submitted our applications. We didn't go, but I did see his signature and I asked who he was. No one, said Jimena.

When I was filling out the forms for Diego to return to Mexico, I finally met the guy and talked to him a little. He gave me his condolences and said nice things about my mom. He gave me the same kind of talking-to I used to give Diego, about how I needed to appreciate what we had. I said yes, and nothing more. I thought it was pretty tasteless of him to try and give me life lessons when it was the first time I'd even met him, and I felt like he was asserting his authority over me just because his ID number was written on my residence card. Yes, yes, whatever you say; yes, yes, whatever you need; just sign and get out of here. But he didn't go—he stayed with my mom and Jimena that day. I locked myself in my room and then I looked him up online. I didn't find much; he was a discreet man with no social media, at least not under his real name. What made him agree to marry Mom? I asked Jimena. I don't know, I guess he thinks he's a good person. But he's not? I asked. Is he? she replied. Well, what do I know, she went on. At least he wasn't like the others, who heard your mom talking about her legal situation with you two so far away, and they'd say how sorry they were and they'd promise to marry her: If you really need it, I would marry you to help you out, they told her. But it was a lie, they never meant it. Your mom asked several of them to follow through, because she really did need it, and they all made up some excuse. That they already had a record, that their partner wouldn't allow it, or whatever. Then why did you offer? your mom would yell at them, but they'd just back away and play the victim, tail between their legs. The Spanish will offer you their house, but they'll never give you the address.

I NEVER KNEW if Diego really did love Jimena. I have the impression that he loved all three of us, and then he didn't. The thing is, his departure feels like such a betrayal, it's hard for me to believe the little bastard ever loved anyone. It's like he cut off my plans for the future, like he maimed me and I was missing an arm or a leg, like I was completely incapacitated from feeling any hope of a worthwhile life. And not because of him, but because he made me see things I'd avoided, made me understand in one fell swoop (crash, boom, bang, Diego hitting the ground) what my place was in the world, and then that stomach pain I had during times of stress became permanent. To live with the gurgle gurgle forever, because the anxiety of living paralyzes you. Because you survive the past, but what about the future—what do you do without a future? Maybe that's what my brother thought and maybe that's exactly why he jumped out the window. What future? It's really cabrón, it's brutal, this having to live for the future because you feel useless in the present and felt miserable in the past. What do you turn toward, how do you live your life when you're carrying all that on your back and have it driving into your stomach? How do you cope alone, with no one to connect with? How do you live in silence with all the noise around you?

And I remember how, when I went to ask Manuela and Carlota for forgiveness, they made me beg for it. They told me that I was the kind of person who only looked for ways to be comfortable, and they were positive that if it were up to me, I would go over to the enemy's side. What fucking enemy, Manuela? What fucking enemy am I going to join? I asked her, almost laughing. There is no enemy! I cried as if declaring the end of a war. Manuela only got more pissed off and told me I just didn't get it, that we had to be united and form alliances, that we couldn't go through life without helping each other, that they needed my loyalty. But what loyalty? I asked. What loyalty are you talking about, how have I ever failed you? When have I not been there for you? Wasn't I the one who made the tea and put the coffee on and sometimes even cleaned the apartment for free? Wasn't I the one who helped you all send money because you didn't know how to use online banking and you didn't know the applications to use to avoid commissions at the locutorios? Wasn't I the one, I asked them, the one who listened to you cry and streamed movies so we could take a break from all the shitty days? Well, they replied, I hadn't joined the cousins in the end, I hadn't committed to the union, I hadn't been right there beside them all the time, I hadn't *been* them. You, the reason you're mad, I told Manuela, is because you think that things have been handed to me, but that's your perspective. I'm not here to tell you everything I've gone through or what I've experienced, because this is not a competition, you know? It's not a competition to see who has suffered more. And as I said that, I felt like I was repeating things my mom had said to me. And there I was, a cartoon version of my mother.

But it was true, I had papers thanks to my mom and I didn't have kids and I didn't have dependents, and I felt like, at least from their perspective, I hadn't suffered as much as them, and they were demanding that I root around in my miseries and bring them into the light and hoist them up like a banner under which we could all be miserable and suffer together, so that we could personify the exact thing that people expected of us. Why don't you fight like this with the college girls who say they're starting the revolution and get all those social media followers, when you're the ones breaking your backs cleaning hotel rooms? Why don't you tell *them* a little less blah, blah, blah, and a little more action? Why don't you think *they're* the ones, with all their time and money, who should band together and do all the things you can't? Why don't you say a word to them, goddammit? I asked. And Manuela got even madder and told me that I really was spoiled, immature, that I only thought about myself, and that she was sure I'd only come to see them because Tom-Tomás didn't love me anymore. What does Tom-Tomás have to do with this? I cut her off. You may not feel any sympathy for me, Manuela, but I was the one who was there at the protests in front of the hotels that fired you all, I was the one who went dancing with you, even when I didn't have the money and couldn't eat the next day; I was the one, Manuela, who got rid of that slimeball who was hitting on you at the bar, and I was the one who walked you home when the fucker started following us. That is friendship, Manuela! The rest of it is fucking bullshit politics and you know it, because everything you've said about the college students behind their backs and everything you've said to my face, you won't say any of it to them, because you know how fast they'll put you in your place. Or weren't they the ones who said first things first, and the first things were *their* demands and *their* priorities and *their* fucking equality? Or weren't they the ones who told you to go to the university to ask for money for the cause and then kept that money saying it was for the host, for the photos, for the poster board? Did you need that poster board, or did they? They need you more than you need them! Why do you even want me to be a cousin when I don't even work at the hotels—you want me to be an imposter like them? Wasn't it Carlota and me who took care of your hand when you spilled lye on it? Or was it the students with their medical insurance? Who took you to the hospital? The college students, or Carlota and me? Who made you laugh? Who cooked you food and who helped you bathe? You want alliances, Manuela, and I want friendship, and that's why I'm here, and that's why I'm apologizing because I really am a pendeja, I *am* a jerk, I told her, and my voice was breaking, because what the fuck with her alliances; what we all needed was to put food in the fridge, not to pose for photos, right? And Carlota grabbed my hand and said yes, that *was* what we needed, and Manuela didn't say anything for a long time, and we sat there at the dining room table, until she sighed deeply, looked straight at me, and said: Let's make arepas for dinner! And we ate well, and that night I stayed over at their house and we made plans to go dancing soon. And that's how I stopped going to the cousins' meetings, and I left the movement.

Then Carlota stopped going too. The thing is, the Spanish students always end up being the spokespeople, and it's all well and good to demand the Convention and human rights and all that, but they don't want to mention immigration law so as not to 'muddy the waters,' she told me. Ultimately, they're the only ones who benefit. And then she opened up and told me about the other issues, but the one that probably bothered her most was the thing with two college girls who were going around saying that one of the cousins was harassing them. And I swear to god it's not true! Carlota told me. What happened was, this cousin put the moves on one of the college girls, and the student took it badly. She didn't tell the cousin straight out, "Hey, I'm not interested, I'm not into you," but instead went to report her and said the cousin was harassing her, and it reached the ears of one of the leaders who'd been around the longest, and instead of listening to the cousin's version of the story, she told her to stop coming to the meetings because she was going to hurt the movement. Can you believe she said that to a woman with three kids in Cochabamba who'd had her job taken away? Just like that, without even asking if it was true, she kicked her out, and this cousin was working on a lawsuit for not getting sick leave. They left her with no legal aid, and no one said a word about it, no one stood up for her. Why didn't she listen to the cousin's version? I asked. Because this woman doesn't like dykes, she said it once: Around here, you can get your tail whichever way you like it, just don't do it in public, or you'll hurt the movement.

Maybe we really are taking all this too seriously. Maybe we just have to stay alive and that's it, said Carlota. I really do get tired of it, she told me. Screw work, screw playing politics. I just want to take it easy and lie on the sand and feel the ocean. Me too, I said, I just want to be surrounded by waves. Let's go! she said. And we spent that whole day at the beach. We went to a shop to buy an umbrella, and some sodas and bread with Spanish omelets from Mercadona, and we went to Somorrostro Beach and did nothing. I remember I sent a photo of the water with my sandy feet to Diego: Look, I've got life figured out, I captioned it. He sent back heart emojis. What are you up to? I asked him. I'm just here, all alone and bored to tears. I'm Diego García, a fucking island, he replied, and added wave emojis. Two weeks later, he killed himself. Once I went back to Madrid, I fell out of touch with Carlota and Manuela. Nothing personal, life is just like that, you're with people when you need to be with them, but in the end you only have yourself.

S OMEDAY YOU WON'T be able to hear me anymore, Diego
told me once when he was little. Diego the prophet. Why
do you say that? I asked the air at my grandparents' house,
only half paying attention because I was watching TV. I always
listen to you, Diego. And he said, Yeah, yeah, and went on playing for a while, then got up and stood in front of me and held his
right hand like a gun and shot some bullets at me. I fell off the
sofa onto the rug. Die, die! Diego shouted, and I pretended to be
dead. He loved to play war, and I let him do it when my grandmother wasn't around to see, because if she caught us, she might
punish us: In a soldier's house, you don't play war.

That day, Diego started to build a fort with pillows and blankets. I'm gonna kill you! he shouted with his gap-toothed grin,
and I made my own hand-gun and pretended to defend myself,
but I always fell down dead and closed my eyes until he came to
give me the final shot, the coup de grâce. I lay like that for like five
seconds, maybe more, waiting for the bang from his mouth before
I writhed around and died for good, but the next thing I heard
was something falling and dishes breaking. Diego had climbed
up onto the china cabinet to jump onto me, but he miscalculated,
and the cabinet fell over on top of him. I was really scared. Diego
had cuts on his forehead and hand, and almost all my grandmother's china broke. The gurgle gurgle in full force. My god,
Diego, what did you do! And Diego cried and cried and I was ter-

rified and didn't know what to do. I tried to clean him up, but the bleeding wouldn't stop. I had to call my grandparents, who had gone shopping at the tianguis. They came as fast as they could and as soon as my grandfather saw my brother with his forehead split open, he put Diego in a taxi and took him to the hospital. I stayed with my grandmother. At first, she didn't say anything, and I started to clean up the broken dishes and tried to sweep. My grandmother was in the kitchen putting away the things they'd bought and when I went to grab the dustpan she started to scold me. What were you thinking? Well, nothing, Abuela, obviously nothing, we were playing. She slapped me. Are you stupid or what? No, I said, now more worried about her reaction. Don't talk back to me when I'm talking to you! And another slap in the face. What were you thinking? He's a child! she screamed at me. I know he's a child, I know, I'm the one who takes care of him and I'm a child too! My grandmother turned into my uncle: She started to hit me with the soup ladle and I tried to run out of the kitchen, but she chased me and yanked my hair and yelled at me. I don't even want to remember what she said, but she made it very clear that I was an idiot and that I could have killed my brother. I wish your mother hadn't had you two, if she wasn't going to take care of you! And I cried and cried and kept talking back, I always talked back, I couldn't keep quiet. Maybe you shouldn't have had her either! And more slaps for me. I don't want to be responsible for anyone! I told her. I don't want to live in this house, either, or have this life! I'm a person too, I hate you, I hate you all! And my grandmother slammed my head hard against the wall. Then I felt dizzy and lost my balance. I don't remember what else happened, or I don't want to. What I do know is that they sure didn't take me to any doctor, even though blood trickled out of my ear. My aunt Carmela brought me some pills for the pain because I told them I felt like I was losing my balance, though my grandmother didn't believe me. Aunt Carmela came to see me every afternoon and put some potato slices on either side of my forehead and said it would help the pain go away. Eventually, it did. My grandmother and I never talked about that. We pretended it had never happened. But my mom found out because Aunt Carmela told her. Mom figured I must have had something wrong with me before, and that my grandmother's beating had just brought it to light.

I NEVER WORRIED too much about my bad hearing. But back in Madrid, after what happened with Diego, I started getting dizzy spells again, and often. My mom told me I needed to see a doctor, because it could be something serious. Then she washed out my ears, and it hurt a lot. My stomach churned as soon as I saw her with the bottle of hydrogen peroxide. But she claimed it was the only way to unclog my ears and cure my vertigo. I was the one who got scolded about it by the doctor. Why would you do that? he asked me, seeming horrified. Then he ordered more in-depth exams, and it took six months to get an appointment. When I finally went in, they asked if I had gotten treatment in Mexico, and I just told them the truth, though modified: that when my ear was infected and leaking pus, I took antibiotics, and it was a long time before things cleared up. And they didn't tell you if it was congenital? Then they started on the tests and warned me that it was more serious than I'd thought, and that I would likely someday lose my hearing permanently.

I F YOU GET diagnosed with chronic deafness or whatever, ask
the doctor if it counts as a chronic disability; if it does, we
won't have to worry about your papers anymore, my mom said,
because you could stay dependent on me, and maybe they'd even
give you some money. I made a face at her. I didn't want to ask the
doctor anything, or seem like a freeloader. What do you think is
going to happen to you when your residence permit runs out and
you don't have a job? What are you going to do then? Have you
thought about that? I hadn't thought anything, and my mom was
right. What made me mad was her attitude, her way of being, how
she made me feel doubly useless: for being deaf and for being an
idiot who didn't know how to build a future for myself.

THE TIME I talked to Marina about Diego, she did seem sad, and she tried to convince me that her classmates were suffering, too. It's hit us hard, she told me. We all thought he was a really smart person, that it was only a matter of time before he adapted. Who's *we all*? I thought. We *all*? Because the few times I went to that school, I left it angry at how most of the teachers seemed to be living in a different era. They didn't understand anything: not us, or any of the others. They were stuck in some world where authority was more important than respect. Or where respect was a synonym for authority. I remember how at one of the parent–teacher conferences, every time the parents asked about homework, about behavior, about curricula, it was always the same answer: Anyone who doesn't comply will be suspended. And that's how it was with everything. What if my daughter this: we'll suspend her. What if my son that: he's suspended. If whatshisname does whatsoever: suspended, suspended, suspended. And it was very much a public school, but they still had Religion as a subject. And there's no other option? Yes, Ethical Values, but it was the same thing: the State, we venerate the State. Really and truly. The worst part was that they wouldn't accept criticism. I remember how that day I asked: Isn't there any way to integrate them instead of kicking them out? You're too young to understand, the guidance counselor told me, this is what it's like with teenagers, either we remove the troublemakers or they hold the entire group back. And isn't there some possibility that it's the pedagogy or the teachers that are failing here? No. Just like that, categorically: no. They were right, everyone else was wrong. And if that wasn't respected: guilty, guilty, out with the outcasts.

MOISÉS SAYS HE AND HIS PARENTS are only passing through here, Diego told me once. Where do they want to go? To Berlin, because maybe there his mom's medical degree would be recognized, and she could practice. And what's keeping them here? Permits. Oh, forget it then, I said, a little teasingly. I'd really like to go to Berlin, maybe things are different there, said Diego. The problem isn't just Spain, I told him. The problem is that you're not European. New York, then. I'll go to New York. But New York was not Diego's destiny either, even if in theory he *was* American.

So what are you going to do? Diego asked me in my dreams, leaning in through my window and trying to pull me out with him. What are you going to do? he asked, and I clutched the rainbow blanket to keep from falling. And I was scared because I knew that he had jumped and I didn't want to see him dead, so I screamed and screamed until I woke up all agitated. Who knows what was worse, waking up or staying asleep.

I ALSO USED TO steal money from Mom when I was a kid. I never told Diego about that, but there it is. Mom worked at a bakery back then, first as an assistant of some kind, then as a department manager. That was important, because my grandfather hadn't sent her to school for as long as she would have liked. What for, when she's just going to have some man supporting her? And my mom worked from Sunday to Sunday, with one day off during the week, which she sometimes spent sleeping, literally, just sleeping: she got up at noon to pee and then went back to bed, without eating, just sleeping. And that was when I'd steal her card from her wallet. More than a few times I snuck out to take money from the ATM at the bank two blocks away: twenty pesos here, fifty there. More than a few times. And I know she never caught me because once, when we went to the mall and she took out money, she said, Ugh, my boss told me he was going to pay my overtime, and he didn't. He did, though; I just kept that overtime for myself.

My mom never liked technology, not phones, not computers, not even microwaves. Even once we were in Madrid, I saw how she'd still rather heat water for her tea in a pot on the stove than put a mug in the microwave. I hate those damned gadgets! she'd say. And I took advantage of that, I took a lot of money that way— between commissions and overtime hours, I always had money in my pocket. Then my mom left for Madrid; I don't know who put that idea into her head, but later I learned that she'd thought about it a lot, debating between Spain and the United States, but someone told her it was easier to enter Spain as a tourist, which was true. It makes a difference if you arrive by plane rather than crossing a desert or ocean. You're still treated badly, but you're not segregated from the start, and at least you have your three months in Schengen territory to figure out how you're going to make it work. In the United States you get six months, but there's the language barrier and my mom doesn't know English, that's why she always paid for Diego and me to take lessons. You two should be able to go where you want, without the pinche language being an obstacle, Mom would say. I took money off her that way, too. If the girl who taught us English charged fifty pesos an hour, I told Mom it was seventy-five. And that's how I was, always: a profiteer. Diego didn't know that.

I do remember how my mom used to say she wanted to leave Mexico, but I didn't take it seriously because people say a lot of things, especially my mom, who has that cruel humor that just pours out of her. As if she had irony coursing through her body, through her stomach, and she's just spitting it out, not because she's evil, but because it's her nature; that's how my mother is, and it took me years to understand that. Every time we fought, she'd tell me: Not everything is about you! I'm a person too! I don't wake up every morning and think about how I'm going to ruin your day! And me: Yes, it *is* about me! You hurt me! I hate you! But I never hated my mother, I just didn't understand her. I didn't understand her, and I didn't try to. That's why, when she said she wanted to leave Mexico, I thought: Oh, right, sure she does. Though she's scared of planes, though she's ugly as sin, though my grandparents think she's incapable of anything. I underestimated her, and when I saw how strong she was, how strong she was without me, I got really angry. But then I realized the contempt she had for her world: Look at this fucking bakery, these guys who go around with drivers and bodyguards, and they throw us a party in this fucking hall with its tin roof. My mom got really mad when the bakery held its employee Christmas dinner at some rinky-dink event hall. I think that was what triggered her hatred for Mexico. You work twelve hours a day so those people can live the good life, and then they give us Styrofoam cups and plastic forks! She spent the whole party complaining like that to one of her coworkers. And the others didn't understand her, either. They told her to be grateful, that almost no other company threw holiday parties like that, but my mom kept going: Fucking bloodsuckers, they feel sorry for us, the sons of bitches.

Before we left for Madrid, I asked my grandfather if we could go to the bakery where my mom had worked, and he took me and Diego there. I wanted one of the cakes my mom used to bring us on weekends, the mocha café kind. Delicious, but we'd gotten sick of it after eating it for weeks on end. I guess I wanted closure or something, and I felt like eating a slice of that cake to celebrate that the three of us were going to be together again. But the bakery no longer existed. It had been on Insurgentes Sur, near San Ángel. It was something else now, I think they sold bathroom tiles. I felt bad. I'd really wanted to tell my mom: So, we went to the bakery and the cakes weren't as good anymore, they don't taste the same without you. But there was nothing left. I told her anyway that we'd tried, and she said, Good, I'm glad they closed, I hope they went broke, fucking bloodsuckers, they were shameless about stealing our time, I'm glad they went broke, I'm glad they're not there anymore.

JIMENA ALWAYS used to say that we Mexicans were some real crybabies. Oh, you all sure do like to whine, she'd tell us. In Mexico you have everything, the best natural resources in the world, and you sit around all lazy and getting fat. That's not true, Jimena, don't say that, there are a lot of poor people, I'd say. And what about in my country, kiddo? Food was rationed in Cuba, and sometimes there wasn't enough to go around. Lines and lines for hours and hours just to go back home with nothing. Did you ever go through that? And we started competing to see who was poorer, and that's why we got so annoyed by Jimena's friends who talked about the shortages during the Spanish Civil War. Oh, my grandfather, he suffered so much, they'd say. We were so poor. We? laughed Jimena. Those were your grandparents, not you. Choose your pronouns well, honey, around here we yank out our own eyes to see who can win Most Miserable, and you're going to lose. With her wit and eloquence, Jimena always won; she always put us in our places, and always with a laugh. Jimena did everything with a laugh and a hug. That's why when people ask if Jimena is my mom, I say yes: I have two mothers. Madrid did give me that.

WHAT ABOUT MY DAD? When are you going to tell me who my father was, when are we going to talk about that? I asked my mom. And she looked at me in surprise. What do you want to know? Well, the truth. What truth? Oh, Mom, whatever it is, I don't know anything. The truth is that you don't have a father. Haven't you been going around saying that Jimena and I are your moms? Where does a damn father fit in there, what do you even need one for? Well, I just want to know. But my mother never told me her story; she said she didn't want me using her past to point any psychoanalytic fingers at her. It is what it is, she insisted. Don't go looking for answers. Nor would she say whether she'd been raped. If we all say we were raped, then no one was raped, understand? No, I told her, I don't understand. We've all had something stolen from us and we are all stealing, she went on. Understand? No, I don't understand you! Well, that's on you, she told me curtly. And I know I take after her because I'm the same way: my truth is always on me.

I REALIZED THAT there was no truth, just points of view. For example, I see very few nice things around me, like everyone I see is out to get me and I am fighting all of them. That's how I picture myself: I walk down the street and look at the people sitting out on terraces and I'm zapping them all. I'll zap you for being racist, you for being a dumbass gilipollas, you just because, you because you talk loud, you because you gave me a dirty look, you, you, you. Everyone gets hit, no one's safe, not even me. Whack, whack, whack. But then they'll tell me I'm a savage, a barbarian, a Mexican. Or a Colombian, and they'll stick a finger up my ass to see if I'm transporting drugs. Because that's how it was when I went to take Diego to Mexico, everyone else was fine at security, next, next, but you, we need to check you. Why me? Them's the breaks, it's just random. But why precisely me, what is suspicious about me? Easy now, kid, don't make things difficult. But what did you see in my suitcase that was strange, what are you looking for? This is all routine. Well of course it's routine, it's extremely routine, that's why I'm arguing, so you'll realize how fucked up it is. A person keeps quiet when she thinks she could lose something, but I had already lost my brother, why would I be quiet? Quiet now, and go over there! And they sent me to another guard who played dumb, who acted like he was checking my things. If I'm going to my own country, why do you even care? Hatred in my eyes. A whack upside his head in my mind, a whack upside everyone's head. Why are you always so angry? my mother used to reproach me. Why *aren't* you angry? That's the real question!

And it was more of the same back in Mexico, nothing but frustration. But I did keep quiet there, because I *did* have something to lose, including my life. And what assurance did I have that my grandmother wouldn't fly off the handle again, or that my uncle wouldn't take his hatred for his wife out on me when he came to visit? What would protect me from Aunt Carmela's husband? Once, at a family dinner, I was wearing jeans and a tight T-shirt, and he ran a finger down my waist and said: Look at you, pretty skinny but all grown up. It was what it was, no one had to explain it to me; I know what I felt and that's why I got out of there fast and never wanted to be around him again, or see him, not even when we were looking for Aunt Carmela and her kids. Even less then, because I'd already known just how culero and malignant he could be.

Silent, then, always silent. Even though the college girls at the cousins' meetings had always told us: Don't keep quiet, your silence hurts us all! Even if silence was what had kept us alive. For me, at least, silence isn't just a precaution. Silence about the soldiers who didn't do anything to me, but who destroyed everything around me. And maybe that's the power of silence: it keeps you isolated, makes you into an island that survives in spite of the waves of fools crashing all around you. No whacks, no zaps, just silence, like the silence that's taking over my right ear, and, the ENT doctor says, will sooner or later also take over the left. Silence.

WHY WOULD YOU speak to me that way, when you know how much I cared about your brother? Marina asked me the time I went to see her at school so she could give me Diego's things. I don't know if you want them, she'd said, and I don't mind keeping them. I want them, Marina, it's best for me to have them. And she gave me a Yankees cap that my grandfather had given Diego, and his Language textbook. I don't know whether it was the stolen one or the replacement, but I felt awful. Thanks, Marina. I wasn't trying to be mean, that's just how I talk. It's ok, she said, sounding sad. I loved him, you know? I really loved him, but not the way he needed. I loved him as a friend more than anything else. Uh-huh, ok. But now I dream about him every night and I can't sleep, she told me. I'm sorry, Marina, was the only thing I could say, because if only I could dream about him, too, instead of just seeing his body in its eternal crash, boom, bang.

Look, that's Bolivia, she said, pointing to a kid who was average-looking except for his hateful eyes. I stared at him and wanted to march over and say: Fuck you, pendejo. But I fought off the urge and it added to the gurgle gurgle in my stomach. Thanks, Marina. Have a good life. But we can chat whenever you want, you can write me, she said, wanting to keep talking, but now my attention was on Bolivia, and I followed him to La Vaguada Park and watched him laughing with his friends, and who knows what they were saying but you could see their roars of laughter and their youth and all that my brother would never get to be. I leaned against a tree to watch them live, all of them. Breathing, the blood running through their veins, their organs functioning full steam ahead. There they were as if nothing had happened, as if my brother had never walked the earth with them, as if he had never existed. And I felt like going up to them, and I even pictured it: marching over and giving them each a big smack upside the head. But what was I going to say? You, for stealing my brother's book, you for this, you for that. No, I kept it all in my stomach; I wasn't about to be the violent Latin American, the fucking savage, the one who reenacted the very system of violence she was trying to escape.

ONCE, JOANA INVITED SEVERAL CLASSMATES, including me, to a slumber party at her house. I don't remember why, but we all told her we would go and then we didn't. Ruth and I, knowing we had no intention of going, still promised to bring ice cream. But I don't remember having done it maliciously, or as a prank, we just did it. Joana was there with the popcorn popped, her mom making dinner, and the movie ready on the TV, but no one showed up. In fact, I still remember how the next time I saw her, I talked to her normally because I didn't understand that we'd hurt her feelings. What's wrong, Joana? And Joana looked at me with contempt and wouldn't talk to me. Then I went and asked Ruth what her problem was. We didn't go to her slumber party! Only then did I catch on. And I regretted that meanness, but I didn't apologize, I let it go. We are especially cruel when we're not trying to be.

Over time, Joana started speaking to me again. We'd left grade school and were freshmen in high school by then; she went to classes in the afternoon and I went in the morning. I was almost always in a hurry because I had to go pick Diego up, and I only managed to say Bye, Joana! And she'd say Bye!, with a smile, as if that meant we were friends again. But the reality is that we were never close, and it's not even that I didn't like her, it's just that I never forgave myself for what I'd done and I was always a little condescending to her. Hi Joana, what are you up to? I'd ask when

I ran into her at the store or the park or wherever, and she, still with that childish smile, would tell me what she was up to. Maybe that was what exasperated me about her, the childishness that she never lost over the years. Oh, she's a little dumb, Ruth would tell me, and I didn't say I agreed, though I did. You just have to smile at the dummies, you know, Ruth said, and we smiled.

Then, when Joana started going out with a friend of Ricardo's, Ruth gave her the same spiel: don't have anything to do with Ricardo, don't talk to him, his dad is evil. My boyfriend isn't bad, Joana said, he's not responsible for what Ricardo's dad does. Joana was the one who told me that Ricardo's dad was a narco. But he's military, I said. But also a narco, she said. Who told you that, Joana? Don't be dumb, you can't believe everything people say. I'm *not* dumb, everyone knows, even your grandmother, everyone knows it. And if you know that, why would you date someone who's so close to narcos? I asked. It's not my boyfriend's fault what Ricardo's dad does! When I remember that, I think she could still be alive today: if we all knew, why didn't we say anything?

M Y GRANDMOTHER TOLD ME that what happened with Joana put everyone on the military base at risk. Everyone looked at themselves in the mirror: they could be the next woman to disappear, or they could have the next woman-killer in their house. No one was safe. Everyone looking at each other sideways to see who had the longest tail and would get it stepped on first.

A lot of women told Joana's mom that bodies turned up in the Remedios River, that she should go and look there. And she did. It turned out that one of the men who had killed lots of girls was in the military. Connections were made, but there was nothing concrete to tie those cases together. And Joana? Disappeared. Even after they turned her body over to her mother, Joana was still disappeared. Her mother said: No, no, that's not my daughter, and people said yes, yes it was, that she should leave it alone, and Joana's friends were carrying her coffin and wailing, but her mom said, No, that isn't my daughter. That's why her brother kept investigating and pulling strings and paying people off, and he found out his mother was right. That body wasn't her daughter's. Joana was still disappeared. You think I'm going to find Carmela, just because I know she was taken and I know who took her? I'm not going to find her, said my grandmother. We're not going to find them, not Joana, not your aunt, not your cousins. Now do you get it that death isn't the worst thing? Or do you have to disappear yourself before you realize? Go to Madrid. Go now.

J OANA ONCE GAVE me a silver ring. She told me it had been a gift from her dad, who had died in a narco ambush in a field in Michoacán. But why would you give this to me? Because we're friends, she said. But your dad gave it to you. And that's why you're going to take good care of it, right? And I kept it. Because it really was pretty, made of silver from Taxco, fine and elegant. A few days before what happened at the military base with Aunt Carmela and the hanging bodies, I took some white lilies to Joana's mom. I put the ring in with them, wrapped in a little box. This is for you, I said. Her mom didn't know about the ring, so I told her the story, and she started crying and thanked me and hugged me really tight while I was trying to put on my raincoat before leaving her house. What a good friend you are! she told me, and all I could get out was an, Oh. But Joana and I weren't really friends. That's why I think it's hypocritical for me to feel bad about her death, and that's why I couldn't ask Bolivia to apologize to my brother's memory.

W E HAD A DOG TOO, same as Ricardo. Not many people had dogs in those days. They were rare on the military base, I guess because the apartments were small and there wasn't room. But we did have one: Flaco. One day he just followed my grandfather home, and he never left again until he died of old age. Flaco was already on his last legs when he came to us, all flea-ridden and mangy. My grandfather and Diego bathed him and took him to the vet. My grandmother didn't pay much attention to him, she didn't like how much he shed, but Flaco stayed with us until he died. And I remember it well, because we all felt bad about it, but Diego suffered the most. My brother was little and always had the dog with him. Flaco, come; Flaco, heel; come, Flaco, Flaquito, Flaquito—we heard that all day in the house. Abuela, give my food to the dog, I'm full. And our grandmother would say no, that in fact, if Diego didn't eat everything, Flaco wouldn't get any food either. That was how we got my brother to eat without complaining.

But Flaco didn't last long; nothing in that house lasted long. Me, it was like I blocked him out; as soon as I saw he was sick, I turned a blind eye and stopped talking to him or petting him. Just like with Diego's dad: as soon as I saw they were more on the other side than this one, I drew a line. No closer, the pain will not come any closer; I shielded myself. But Diego, yes, Diego did let the pain in. I remember how maybe two nights before Flaco died,

Diego lay on the floor and talked to him: You've lived a good life, Flaco, you made us happy. You can die, you don't need to suffer anymore. It gave me goosebumps. I should have paid attention to my brother then, and maybe I did, and maybe I also drew a line with him later and knew enough to leave for Barcelona in time, to get far away from him because I knew he was going to die.

ONCE, DIEGO CAME HOME REALLY STONED. You could tell because he was all gangly by then, but he seemed even clumsier than usual, knocking things over and moving in slow motion. My mom got really mad and yelled all kinds of things at him. Jimena wasn't there that day. Oh, this kid is some kind of pendejo! my mom said. And Diego laughed with his big teeth biting his lip because he couldn't even talk. Is he high? Mom asked. I shrugged. Just what I needed, for him to be a pothead! And me: Well, better a pothead than a dealer. What are you talking about? she chided me. But I was being serious—it was better for him to be caught smoking than selling. If he was dealing it would be jail time for sure, I had no doubt about that. But my mom didn't understand my logic and said: Don't stick your nose where it doesn't belong, cabrona, it's none of your business, don't encourage this little brat who thinks I go to work just so he can fuck around. So I didn't stick my nose in. At least not with Mom. She lectured us for a long time about how her family had been in danger for years because of exactly this kind of shit. Everyone is threatened, there's a war, and you two think drugs are nothing but fun and games! Diego laughed. What are you laughing at? What do you think your uncle goes to Guerrero or Michoacán for, vacation?

Then I did try to go talk to Diego, but I overheard him

talking to someone on the phone. He was asking her if she was in bed, if she was wearing a shirt, if she wanted to fuck him. It really threw me off, and I left that little jerk for my mom to deal with. After all, I thought, she's his mother, he's her problem. I drew my line.

FTER A WHILE, we decided to move. Living in the place where Diego had died was bad for us. It took us time to decide. Mom and I both wavered. On one hand, we agreed that yes, moving was for the best; on the other, the gurgle gurgle in our stomachs held us back. Leave the last place Diego had existed? We were paralyzed, but Jimena was there for us. She took us to La Prosperidad, said we would like it there. The name seemed like a joke: Prosperity, in Madrid. Jimena had even gotten Mom a job in El Viso, at a nursery school. Full time, legal, stable. Jackpot. I never saw my mom in mourning—not even the day I came from Barcelona did she skip work or miss taking care of whoever she was caring for that day. On the contrary, from then on she pushed herself to work harder, as much as she could, to keep her mind occupied, and that's why Jimena was so excited about the new job. It'll be good for her, she said, paid vacation and everything—she didn't even get that at the bakery. And what are you going to do? she asked me. You have to decide. I'm going to live in La Prospe too, I told her, in pure prosperity. But she didn't like my irony. You're not going to do what your mom wants? she kept asking. Do what she wants? But we've already proved her right! And we had, because she'd always said it loud and clear: Do you want to stay like this forever, in this room, this house, this city? You don't want that, even if you think you do, you don't want that. My mom flying, from Mexico to Madrid. My mom landing in El Pilar and then El Viso and La Prosperidad, shabby and beaten, but solid. My mom being my mom, in her inner monologue, emerging victorious and escaping the filth that neither Diego nor I could leave behind.

I TRIED. Not so much with myself, but with Diego. I gave as much as I could, I pushed myself all the time. I followed the rules and held his hand for years. I swear I tried. I try with myself, but I just can't. There's nothing that seems worth fighting for; my residency card is going to expire soon and there are no appointments to process another one. Jimena says we're going to try everything, but that I have to tell her what it is I want, and then I have to do it. Do you want to sew, to clean, to study? What? Do *something*. But I don't want anything. I spend most of my time in my room thinking about Diego and looking at a photograph of us together: my hair is in braids and I'm wearing a flowered dress that I didn't like but that Diego's dad had bought me, and Diego still has a pacifier in his mouth, his curls tousled and his hands clutching my skirt. Come on, let me take a picture of you two like that, our grandfather had said, and he'd printed it so I could take it to Mom at her mother-in-law's house. But Mom didn't want it. I don't want to look at Diego, he's just like his dad, I don't want to. So much like his dad: fleeting. So I hold on to that photo, because like Diego said, your name is your destiny, and I see our names written in pencil on the back. We are still those little kids: frightened and confused children who won't ever have a chance.

WHAT HAPPENS TO a dream deferred? The one that never reaches you because there's a nightmare stuck in your brain and it won't let you sleep? Does it rot, does it stink? Maybe it stays mired in your head, or in your stomach, like a heavy weight that you can't digest. Or else it explodes, and it's your guts that rumble at midnight. It doesn't matter how soft your pillow is, the nightmare never stops. It's a loop. Like the song on repeat in your head that you can't get rid of. It's Vampire Weekend on Diego's phone, their sickly sweet little tunes. It's Diego's music permeating my brain because I know that someday I'll never be able to hear it again. What happens to dreams that don't exist? They jump out the window over and over and over and over, until you want to jump out the window too, but Ezra Koenig sings again and the playful music prevails. Again and again, over and over. Ezra, window, Ezra, window, until it becomes absurd but real.

I F YOU COULD know what day you were going to die, would you tell me? No, of course not, don't be silly, Diego. Why do you think about that kind of thing? I'm curious, he said. It's just out of curiosity, but think about it—would you tell me? What for? I asked. What if I would want to know? he insisted. I don't know, Diego, it's really shitty to think about that, real culero of you to ask that question. Did you know that Vampire Weekend is going to play in Mexico? he asked. No way! And they're not coming here? Not that I've seen. What would you say to the singer? Nothing, he replied. Muah, muah, muah, I made the sound of mocking kisses. Pendeja, he said, but his voice broke, I heard it. What's wrong, Diego, did you fight with Mom? And Diego couldn't speak, he had something stuck in his throat, I guess. Are you crying because you're not going to see Vampire Weekend? And a quick laugh from my brother. Asshole, he said, clearing his throat. Muah, muah, I love you, Ezra Koenig. And I like to think Diego was smiling; I want to believe that he did smile. I gotta go, pendeja, he said. Ok, talk soon. We hung up.

Two hours later the phone rang again, but I didn't hear it. Then he called again, and I still didn't hear. Two more calls from his phone are registered in mine. The fifth time it rang it wasn't my brother anymore but an unknown number, and it called back many times until finally I saw the screen and answered and a voice talked to me about Diego. I didn't see him, but it's as if I'd seen him, because I have the image drilling into my head and it won't let me sleep. Always the same image: Diego falling and the sound of his body when it hits the ground.

ACKNOWLEDGMENTS

To Alejandra Eme Vázquez, for being there at the start of this fiction's gestation.

To Laura Ramos Zamorano, for being with me at every moment of the novel's writing and supporting me with her critical reading.

To Yuri Herrera, Jimena Gorraez, Emiliano Monge, Alexandra Saavedra, and Daniela Rea, for their reading: thank you always.

To Benjamin Russell, for being the king of the sports.

To my daughters, who give me the time I am not with them.